Jane's Special Adventure

Lori Laidlaw

Published by Lynda French, 2024.

JANE'S SPECIAL ADVENTURE

First edition. March 26, 2024.

ISBN: 978-1998074280

Written by Lori Laidlaw.

To those who choose to explore consensual non-monogamous love...

Introduction

About *"Jane's Special Adventure"*

Jane discovers her sex appeal in a polyamorous relationship with three young professionals. Her epiphany shows she's always allowed herself to be overshadowed by her childhood bestie Olivia, whose star shines so much brighter.

Life goals, career expectations, and the demands of friendship collide with red-hot desire as jealousy gets mixed up with love, betrayal, and narcissistic behavior.

While the two women and three men revel in their erotic escapades the five struggle to hold on to their friendship. Can they make their way forward together? Find out in this steamy, multiple POV, modern coming-of-age story.

Re-written from the original "Secrets, Secrets", published in 2023, this 30k+ novella is distributed wide.

Playlist

"All About That Bass" by Kate Davis

"Boom Boom" by John Lee Hooker

"Drive" by The Cars

"D'yer Mak'er" by Led Zeppelin

"Feva for the Flava" by Hot Action Cop

2

"Fever" by Rita Coolidge

"God Only Knows" by The Beach Boys

"Samba Pa Ti" by Santana

"Sex and Candy" by Marcy Playground

"Sexy, Sexy, Sexy" by James Brown

"The Seed" by The Roots

"Wild Thing" by Fancy

Chapter One

Jane

"Damn, I hate having to lie to Livy's mother again. The woman is tenacious, she just won't let up. But that's it, I'm done!

No more keeping Livy's secrets. I've been doing it since we were five years old and got Lonnie Kegenbauer in trouble by lying over who ate the maple sugar cookies in kindergarten class.

I didn't even like the taste of those cookies so Livy ending up eating them all. She greedily stuffed her face because she was never allowed to eat sweets at home. Then she made me join her in pointing the finger at Lonnie.

Not that I felt sorry for him, he was a mean kid and the teacher believed us. Well, she believed Livy because Livy was the teacher's pet. She got to sit in the middle of the front row and hold the guinea pig for the class picture.

I'm the first to admit Livy was a beautiful child and is now a beautiful woman, but I've been living with the fact that Livy has always been everybody's favorite for almost twenty years now. It was probably in our adolescence that girlish envy turned into jealousy and maybe more... but she's my best friend and I love her.

Still, I'm the last person she should be asking to keep her secrets!

Miss Kitty

Most of the strippers choose hard rock so they can bump and grind to its pounding rhythm but Miss Kitty is different. She picks the romantic melodies popular for slow-dancing at Prom Nights in the Fifties and

Sixties. She moves gracefully across the stage, swaying and swiveling her hips. Seductively elegant, ultra-feminine, every man's desire.

Miss Kitty adores the spotlight and thrives on the applause and cheering. Her black catsuit is skintight and the latex glistens under the lights. Balancing perfectly on one impossibly high-heeled shoe she slowly lifts her right leg until it's fully extended straight up. Reaching out she grabs hold of the zipper tab at her ankle and pulls it to her hip. The material falls open revealing smooth, pale skin. The audience roars with approval.

Miss Kitty then repeats the performance with her other leg and now dances with the fabric fluttering around her limbs. She languorously unzips the sleeve from wrist to shoulder baring first one arm and then the other. The crowd urges her to keep going, keep going!

She continues to seduce them with alluring and erotic dance steps and poses, sinuously twining around the pole, languidly spinning. The guys are tossing coins and bills onto the stage. Miss Kitty revels in the excitement of having all eyes on her, all of the men wanting her.

Next she unzips the costume from her waist to crotch-level then reaches up to the last zipper, the one at her neck. She very slowly starts to pull it down and the audience seems to collectively hold its breath.

After exposing a teasing of cleavage Miss Kitty asks: "Should I continue?"

And the place goes wild with stamping and clapping, whistling and shouting. Lots more money hits the stage. Miss Kitty spins in a circle then dramatically unzips and flings the shirt wide open, her breasts springing free with her nipples hard and enticing.

She turns around and bending down reaches from back to front to grab hold of the zipper at her crotch. She wiggles while she pulls it all the way round and by time she's finished and is completely nude her audience is in a frenzy. She shimmys her hips and looking back, over her shoulder, gives an exaggerated wink. The crowd loves it.

Clad in nothing but heels and a cat mask Miss Kitty performs a couple of sexy, slinky dances strutting from one side of the stage to the other, colored lights bathing her body. Excitement flows from the audience and Miss Kitty delights in the buzz. Showing off she thrusts out her chest and shakes her shoulders to bounce her breasts. She pinches her bottom, she twists her nipples, and she caresses the smooth mound of her pussy.

Twirling and swirling on stage to the claps and whistles and money tosses from the audience is such a heady rush. Miss Kitty knows she was born to perform, to be the star, to be the object of everyone's desire. At this moment in time all that matters to her is that her adoring audience is entranced and entrapped by the allure of her charms. She is a goddess in all her naked glory!

Snaking her arms above her head lifts up her breasts while she smiles and pokes the tip of her tongue between her teeth. Then running her hands all the way along the front of her body down her long legs she bends over to grasp her ankles and slowly spins round giving everyone an exciting glimpse of pink.

As the lights fade signaling the end of her show cash continues to shower the stage. In the dark Miss Kitty and her helpers quickly scoop it up to the drumming of applause and stomping feet then she hurries off to the dressing-rooms.

Miss Kitty is so popular she only has to perform a few times a month to earn enough to supplement her student loan while she completes her graduate studies.

Livy

I've always found that it pays to be a good tipper. You buy goodwill and get great service. Bruno the bouncer always tells me I don't have to give him any money just to get escorted to my limo but I'm grateful for his protection and his loyalty.

Same with my driver, Edwin. He has a grandfatherly attitude towards me and I know he'll always faithfully guard my privacy. He's also savvy enough to keep an eye out for tails when driving me home. I live in student residence so I'm safe once I'm inside the dorm but there's always a chance someone from the audience will try to follow me when I'm en route. Edwin gets a big tip even though he owns the limo business.

Tipping well is just good policy. Plus, it's important to leave a legacy of goodwill on my rise to the top.

I'm a planner. Sure, I've acted impulsively a few times in my life but I've usually regretted those actions afterwards. I needed to supplement my student loan with an income that wouldn't interfere too much with my studies so I researched good-paying jobs for college girls and honestly, these search engines should come with a filter!

The choices were escort, sugar baby, cam girl, and exotic dancer. So, stripper it was but I needed to figure out what was the best way to compete against other pretty naked girls? I realized I had to make the clientele - the audience - really want me and that meant leaving them craving more. I could easily do that by only performing occasionally.

Then I decided I need a hook, a signature move, or a brand. That's when I hit upon the Miss Kitty persona. She doesn't perform to a schedule and she has an enticing aura of mystery. It's paid off big-time.

Jane helped by getting money from her parents telling them it was for me to get portfolio photos professionally done. It was enough to put together the limo and the costume and then apply for the job. Management was impressed and as an actress I certainly know how to get the audience eating out of my hand. So to speak...

I wear a latex cat-suit, a turban fashioned into two cat's ears, and a Lucky Cat mask that comes down over my nose. With deep rose lipstick I reshape my mouth and no one can suss out my identity.

I love performing and can't wait until I'm a famous actor on stage and on film. Of course I won't do any nude scenes. I don't object in principle – obviously, since I adore having men ogle my nude body – but because it's vitally important that I be taken seriously in my career. I don't ever want people to be speculating about whether that was me in the raw or a body-double. Or if I've had some work done. I haven't of course, I'm a factory-original model. All natural, au naturel.

Acting is just the beginning for me. By time I finish my education and gain all I can from practical experience I'll be able to go anywhere in the entertainment field and, when I lose my looks, I'll be able to teach the craft. I hope that time is decades and decades away because I want to enjoy many years on stage and in front of a camera. Just look at Maggie Smith's career!

Acting isn't the most glamorous job but it's certainly the most glamorous profession. Being a star is everything to me and I'm laser-focused on achieving my goal.

After putting on a show I come straight home. I'm always sweaty and hot from the lights and the black turban which covers my hair and the cat mask that hides my face. I'm usually horny, too. Even though I can't really see the audience since they're in the dark and I'm in the light I can definitely sense them. I feel the heat of their bodies, I hear their lusty pleas, and I can certainly imagine their thoughts of what they'd like to do to me. I can't describe what a turn-on that is.

Wrapped up in a raincoat I hustle upstairs to the communal bathroom where I peel everything off then jump into the shower. By time I've soaped up and rinsed off I'm aching to rub my itch. If there's no one around I take care of it under a strong stream of warm water. I always orgasm quickly.

If I don't have privacy in the shower I hurry back to my room and into bed. If Jane's still awake I tell her sorry but I have to deal with my business. She just shakes her head at me.

I never hear Jane masturbate but of course she must. Maybe she can't climax unless she has utter privacy? Or does she stifle her ecstatic cries so her orgasms are politely quiet? That thought makes me chuckle. Poor Jane! When it comes to my body I'm not a private person at all.

Although when it comes to my identity no one knows about my strip-tease persona of Miss Kitty. Except Jane, of course. Jane knows all my secrets.

Chapter Two

Drew

As usual I told myself I would not keep looking over at Olivia Carstairs but my eyes betray me and continue to stray in her direction. And she's perfectly well aware of my gaze even if she doesn't acknowledge me.

Of course she does acknowledge – in subtle, teasing ways – that I'm watching her. Like now. I've been glancing up the length of her long bare legs from her sandaled feet to the hem of her mini-skirt. She isn't looking at me but suddenly she swivels in her seat and her legs are splayed. Her skirt has crept up her thigh and I catch a flash of her white panties. I'm instantly aroused.

She crosses her legs and meets my eyes with an innocent smile that barely conceals laughter. Dammit, I'm the one in charge here! I'm the lecturer and I'm about ten years her senior yet she manages to reduce me to the state of horny adolescence. I have a powerful urge to teach her a lesson she won't soon forget!

I suddenly realize I've stopped speaking for too long. The students are staring at me and I have to fight down this flustered feeling. I'm very young to be a professor of psychology and it's important that I keep my cool and my gravitas and maintain discipline. Uh-oh, the thought of disciplining Olivia Carstairs almost does me in... another distraction!

I end the lecture soon after and wait while the students stream past, exchanging a few comments while biding my time until Ms Carstairs approaches but she's tricked me by going up the stairs and out of the lecture hall by the doors at the top. I can hear her laughter in my head.

Harry

I've really enjoyed spending time with Jane during her practicum. I've taken on several students from the veterinary college over the years and she is definitely my most appealing trainee. She's sweet. It helps that she's the best friend of my heart-throb.

Olivia Carstairs has been my crush for years now. She's gorgeous, smart, funny, mega-personality, and the world's biggest cocktease. Seriously. She knows the effect she has on me and every other guy, too!

Olivia is about 5 foot 9 with most of that height being long legs. She has the unusual pairing of blonde hair with milk-chocolate eyes. A sprinkling of freckles across her nose (makes me wonder where else she has freckles???), adorable dimples, creamy complexion, and a body to dream about. As I do, a lot. I day-dream about her, too.

Anyhow, I was ready to like Jane simply because she might be a stepping-stone to bring me closer to Olivia. As it turns out Jane is a great gal. She's no Olivia but she's still very attractive in an average sort of way.

That doesn't sound very appealing but really she's a nice little package: medium height and weight, well-proportioned body, great rack actually, pretty face with a killer smile, and a very good brain.

She's too shy and her posture needs improving. She needs to push those tits out, lift up her head and walk with pride and self-assurance. A heavy hit of self-confidence would do her a world of good and hmm... I think I can provide it.

Yeah, it's time to let the idea I've got forming come to fruition. It won't be the first time the three of us have done this but it hasn't happened since college. I guess we all got too wrapped up in being serious adults with professions these days but... yeah, we're overdue for some mindless sexy fun but in a safe environment.

It'll have to wait until Jane's practicum is over otherwise it might look like favoritism. That means I've got about a week to finalize my scheme and to enjoy the anticipation!

Brent

I've been told I'm the best looking of the three of us. We've called ourselves the Three Amigos, the Three Musketeers, even the Three Stooges since our friendship formed in elementary school. It continued throughout our school-days and although those are behind us and we're each working in our chosen fields we're still as close as ever.

Drew is a College Professor of Psychology, Harry is a Small Animal Veterinarian, and I'm a Criminal Prosecutor, although I'm very low-level right now.

I've got the Black Irish coloring of black hair, dark blue eyes, and very white skin. I don't tan but I don't sunburn either. I also got through my teens blemish- and acne-free. That's probably why people said I was the handsomest. Well, actually I guess I do have the most male model type of looks out of all of us.

None of us were high-school jocks but we played on our school's teams and still keep fit with swimming, racquetball, skiing, and hiking. Three friends from similar middle-class backgrounds with good educations, promising careers, and a friendly competition to finally score with the one girl we've all been wanting for years: Olivia Carstairs.

I have no doubt that Olivia, Livy as she's called by her cute friend Jane, will be a famous actress someday. Actor, I guess I should say. In addition to being drop-dead gorgeous with a body that won't quit – if that's not too many cliches! she has incredible focus and drive.

We've all enjoyed dates with her but she puts up barriers to keep anyone from getting too close. She's made it clear that she doesn't want to be anyone's girlfriend and she certainly doesn't want to fall in love. She's a party girl who is always up for a good time of drinking and dancing, trivia games and charades, sporting events and activities, but it's always hands-off at the end of the night.

She wants to have fun without attachments and that presents a challenge that none of us three can resist.

The Guys

While growing up, people always lumped Andrew (Drew) Thomas, Harrison (Harry) Fletcher, and Brent Jamieson together because the threesome was such a complete unit. Their friendship was both envied and admired.

They met as cub scouts while still in grade school. As boy scouts they learned to camp, snowshoe, and kayak - each enjoying the outdoor activities. In high-school they dated steadily but none of them ever went steady with just one girl.

Their families referred to them in the collective as the boys and their friends called them the guys. The guys could always be counted on to make up a team or join a party or go on a trip. The guys set standards with their opinions such as Playboy over Penthouse, Rugby over Football, Rock over Alternative music... and they were popular because their self-containment as a trio meant they weren't challenging the top dog in any particular endeavor. The Homecoming King and the Captains of the school's sports teams never felt threatened.

Happy and attractive, fit and healthy, smart and sociable. Harry has the most muscular physique, Drew is the brainy one, and Brent is a strikingly handsome man.

As adults their friendship has only grown deeper. Their companionship is as natural to them as breathing and they're wholly involved in each other's lives, as close as flesh-and-blood brothers.

While still in school they pooled their money and bought a house on Riverside Drive. It's an older building made of brick with a tall skinny shape located near the university and across from the river.

They rented a place together while in college so are very comfortable sharing their home, a home that's skyrocketed in value.

Chapter Three

Jane

Oh he's lucky to live here, I think while looking up at Harry's house. The neighborhood is funky-turned-chic and the properties here are worth a lot. Proximity to the river is a huge attraction, and both the walking and the biking paths are popular. I would love to move into one of these places.

Harry's invitation surprised me because I know how he feels about Livy but I thought I'd only be spiting myself if I refused out of pique. After all, if some of Livy's allure can rub off on me then why not take advantage of it?

I really enjoyed my work-placement at the clinic. I like Harry and he's a great teacher. He's also very easy on the eyes with such a well-built physique.

Not all vets are willing to take on students so I was very fortunate to get hands-on experience with him. I'm halfway through veterinary school, and three-quarters through my eight-year's of training, and I know becoming a vet is the right choice for me.

I knew I would still see Harry from time to time once my training was over because we have mutual friends and interests but I didn't think he'd ask me out on a date. Well, I wouldn't really call it a date... he's lured me over to his place with the latest Mission Impossible movie, just released, and a projector screen to watch it on.

I love the stunts and drama in action movies but don't see many because Livy isn't a fan, and we usually go to the show together. She always complains about such-and-such a thing being impossible to do or something being totally unbelievable and I tell her she has to learn how to suspend belief and immerse herself in order to enjoy the story.

You'd think that would be exactly what an actor could – and would – do but she's got a critic's eye and it's rare that she can just watch a film and enjoy it.

Harry said we'll have lots of popcorn while watching the show but if we're hungry after we can go out for a burger and beer. Not exactly the height of romance but it does mean I don't have to worry about dressing up in this heat. It's been an unseasonably warm Springtime and my shorts and halter-top ensemble will be perfect for a comfy evening at home.

I'm not a very girly-girl so nail polish and false eyelashes aren't my thing, but I do love perfume so I spritzed on some *Romance* my favorite Ralph Lauren scent. There, I think I look good for my role as a movie-watching buddy.

Harry warned me that the neighbors are fighting a bitter battle over parking spaces so I took an Uber over to the house on Riverview and now I'm standing at the front gate admiring his home. I wonder if his house-mates will be home? I know them too, but not as well since they're older and finished at our high-school before I'd begun. But I know of them, and Livy's dated them, and we've been to some of the same social events.

Livy

Jane has a date! At least, I think it's a date. She's being very coy about the guy and what they're doing, telling me it's no big deal. Hmm, that girl needs to go out more.

She's a beauty but she can't or won't see it. I'm beautiful and I know it and I'm glad about it. Life is easier this way. Jane's beautiful too but she acts like she doesn't believe it so she isn't loud and proud. She needs some guy to fall head-over-heels in love to convince her.

Jane claims her self-esteem is fine – and maybe it is in the academic world where her brains count – but she needs the kind of validation only a romance can give. Huh! I'm one to talk.

In my case my ambition and working towards my goals - and finally achieving them - helps me to flourish.

In Jane's case it means she'll need to find love to get some sense of value and completeness. Unfortunately that can also be the road to heartbreak and hurt. Still, it doesn't have to be, and maybe this guy she's sort of going out with tonight will be the one.

Jane's career won't be impeded by having a boyfriend or a husband. Not even when she has a family of her own, as I'm sure she will someday, so if that's her chosen path then the sooner she gets started on it the better.

I love Jane. She's so smart and helpful and kind and compassionate... oh I do hope she's found a good guy! And I hope he's *the one*.

Harry

The movie was great and Jane liked it too, laughing at the jokes and gasping at the suspenseful bits. I like to see a girl enjoying herself. I'm looking forward to more of that starting right now.

That wide-eyed innocent stare and the slight quiver to her body as I tighten my arm around her shoulders is really getting to me. I can't wait to explore that mouth and that body. Her lips, slightly shiny from the buttery popcorn, are ripe for kissing.

Ohhhh, she tastes good. She's so warm and soft and cuddly. Her hair looks frizzy but it's surprisingly soft. Ah, I guess she's naturally curly but blow-dries it straight. Why can't girls be happy with themselves the way Mother Nature intended?

Uh-oh, I let a slight groan escape and I've given her a scare. Time to back off with the caresses and concentrate on providing some expert kissing. Not too hard but hard enough to show passion, not wet and not sloppy, a kiss then a little nibble on her lower lip. Aha! now *she's* the one giving a little groan of pleasure.

I'm justifiably proud of my seductive skills.

Putting my hands at the back of her neck I slowly draw them up against her head with my fingers gently pulling through her hair. The gesture tugs her head back and I start kissing her chin and her throat. A few more strokes through her scalp and then my hands are back at her neck. The two buttons of her halter-top are quickly undone and the fabric falls loose.

I'll scare her off if I move too fast so I shift us around until her back is against my chest. My chin rests on top of her head and I compliment the softness of her hair. I wrap both arms around her, holding her hands, and pull her in close, comfortably warm and companionable. I feel her relax. We both know that the top of her halter is undone, it's only the built-in bra cups that are holding it in place, but I don't make a move and she probably thinks I've forgotten, or it was accidental.

I hear a key in the door and think good, right on time before I tilt Jane's head to the side and start probing her ear with delicate licks and indrawn breaths, guaranteed to send chills down her spine and distract her.

She opens her eyes in surprise when she feels Brent sit down on the couch beside her. He stares into her face and gives her a delighted smile and why not? she looks lovely with her mussed hair, soft mouth, and lips puffy from kissing.

Her chest heaves with a deep breath as she looks into his eyes that sparkle and draw her in. The movement catches his attention and before she can react he's untied the bow that closes the front of her top.

Jane struggles a bit but I'm holding her hands and pinning her arms with my own. This is the crucial time when she either gives in to her excited curiosity or shuts us down with a No! It's only when I exhale as the moment passes that I realize I'd been holding my breath hopefully.

Brent gently pulls her top open, exposing her bare breasts, and studies her with appreciation before once again staring into her eyes and saying: "You're lovely, Jane."

She is, too. Her breasts are round and full with the faint blue lines of veins showing through her milky white skin. Pale pink nipples are darkening as they harden under his gaze.

It's like she's mesmerized. Brent reaches out to stroke one breast while I cup my hand around the other, hefting the weight of it in my palm. Her skin is so soft and warm.

Again Jane moves as if she's thinking she should get away but between my arms and Brent's eyes we're holding her captive. She doesn't struggle too hard and she doesn't say a word.

All I can hear is her breathing, and Brent's, and my own, all growing more voluble as we massage and caress and pinch. Brent leans down to kiss each breast and rub his face against her tender flesh. She gasps an oh! while a flush of excitement blossoms across her chest.

Deftly pulling the halter-top free of our bodies Brent now has Jane naked from the waist up and visibly aroused. His fingers tickle their way down her belly to the buttons of her shorts. Jane murmurs something, surely not a protest? because when Brent kisses her mouth she lifts her body to meet his. I reach my hand between them and finish the unbuttoning.

Brent discarded his suit jacket when he came in, he worked today, and now he pulls back to loosen his tie and undo a few buttons to drag his shirt over his head. It's always a surprise to see such white skin on a man who has to shave his beard twice a day. He's currently sporting a dark five o'clock shadow and his grin gives him the look of an amiable pirate.

He certainly has Jane hypnotized. Her eyes rove over his toned physique following the line of black hair that moves down his abs through the vee of his hips before disappearing beneath the pants of his suit.

Brent continues where I left off and slides Jane's shorts and panties down over her thighs before sweeping them off in one quick gesture. Jane seems embarrassed when we see her pubic hair but we both exclaim with pleasure at the nest of auburn curls.

"So pretty!" says Brent as he drinks in the sight of her lying bare-naked between us.

Jane makes a halfhearted attempt to cover her privates but we don't allow that, we want to enjoy the view. Brent is crouched between her thighs while she reclines against me and I'm lying back on the couch.

I lift her arms up over her head exposing her like an offering. The position forces her big breasts to jut out and emphasizes the deep indent of her waist before flaring out to the curve of her hips. She's utterly delectable.

I've been too preoccupied to hear Drew come in but suddenly he's pulled up a chair and leaning in says: "Oh good, dinner-and-a-show."

That's when I notice he's brought a bucket of chicken and a big bag with all the fixings that he puts down on the coffee table.

Brent flips the lever on the side of the couch which drops the back down and turns it into a fold-out bed. "Come and join us," he says with a conspiratorial smile.

Drew replies: "Oh, I will, but first I want to watch for awhile. Jane! I love your curly pubes, and look at those nipples, they're like hard little red rubies!"

Jane

I don't know what I'm doing! I think in a panic. I'm stark naked with three men in the room and we're kissing and they're touching me and taking their clothes off. I'm loving it and hating it at the same time.

I mean, it feels wonderful and they're so gentle and so nice and so well... *loving*. It doesn't feel in the least bit wrong but it is wrong and I know it's wrong.

This kind of intimacy should be one-on-one not shared, and yet... it feels so good and the way they're looking at me feels pretty good, too. I wonder if this is how Livy feels all of the time? Oh damn, I didn't want to think of her right now. I don't want to wonder if these guys are making comparisons in their minds between me and her. They won't want me if that's what they're doing. But they do want me so maybe they aren't... maybe I'm just thinking the worst.

With the couch folded out Harry has moved me to lie on my side between him and Brent. He's stroking my hair and my back, massaging my bum and reaching round to fondle my breasts. His hands move everywhere, gentle but persistent.

All the while I'm drowning in Brent's gorgeous blue eyes. They glitter and sparkle and drown me. He's such a handsome man I just want to stare and stare. Oh, he's pulled off his own shorts and now he's naked and oh my, he's very aroused. Aroused by me. Maybe I have managed to channel a little bit of Olivia Carstairs after all!

Suddenly Brent has managed to put on a condom and lie back pulling me on top of him. I love it. The skin of his chest feels hot and he's holding me so close my boobs are squashed. I slide down onto his dick and as soon as the head breaches my passage I tighten myself around him.

Lifting up I start riding him while his fingers find my clit. The tingling sensation is instant and overwhelming. In my head I hear that old instrumental by Santana that's so exquisitely sensual. I feel sensuous and sexy as hell.

The guys are all watching as I grab my breasts and twist my nipples until they truly are as red and as hard as rubies. I'm so excited I'm gonna burst!

My hips are rocking to their own rhythm and I'm reveling in my sexuality, I'm on top and in charge. I'm the star of this show! And my audience can't resist joining in.

My eyes are closed. Someone is kissing me, someone has taken over massaging my breasts, someone else is squeezing my ass and all the while I'm pistoning up and down on Brent's cock until an orgasm catches me unawares. I cry out with the pleasure and soon after Brent gives a hoarse shout. I'm wet and throbbing but I'm immediately pushed down on my back and entered again, this time by Harry.

Brent has flopped down beside me and the smile in his eyes sends a warmth right through me. I want to smile back but the urgency of Harry's furious stroking claims my attention when he finds my g-spot. I wasn't even sure I had one! but he's hitting something that feels so good. I'm clutching onto to him, rubbing my hands over his biceps – so hard, so muscular, so reassuringly protective.

"I can't hold it," he gasps. I understand that he was holding himself back all the time he spent seducing me. He climaxes and I'm so close to cumming again but Harry is spent. I whine my frustration but luckily Drew is ready to take his turn.

He flips me over and lifts up my hips to have me doggie-style. It's a position that lets him go deep. Brent props himself up so can finger my clit and in moments my hips are gyrating uncontrollably while I briefly go to some other place where I can hear Drew's shout of fantastic! but only faintly.

I'm lost in my own space. I feel nothing but pleasurable sensations vibrating through me that last seconds or minutes – I have no idea – I just know when it's over I'm happily limp and worn out. I lay there weak and helpless and deliciously satiated.

Although I didn't realize it all of the men had put on condoms so they went off one by one to clean themselves up. The four of us are curled on the sofa-bed, languidly stroking each other and bestowing kisses. It's been such a deeply moving experience. I feel warm and protected and I never want it to end.

Harry teases me with his fingers and I whimper. He chuckles and tells me I'm not the only thing that's finger-licking good. That's when I realize I'm starving! We all are, so we dig into the food Drew brought. There's chicken and french fries and gravy and potato salad. It feels like a picnic as we loll on the sofa-bed eating with our hands.

Suddenly I realize that I'm the only one still naked and for some reason this feels shameful. I hurry into the bathroom and get in the shower. I half-hope one - or more! - of the men will join me but they don't. I try, not very successfully, to keep my hair from getting wet since it will get curly and frizzy.

I wash myself thoroughly but I keep soaping up again and again while turning the tap up until the water gets hotter and hotter. I don't feel like I'm getting clean.

When I step out of the shower and look in the mirror I see the same old me but how can that be when I've just let these three men who are practically strangers fuck me and do whatever they want with me?

Drew

When Jane comes back into the room, tightly wrapped in a towel, we can all see that something's wrong. She won't look anyone in the eye and her whole posture isdefeated and unhappy. Brent starts to say something but I stop him. I understand what's happening and I can fix it.

"Jane come here and sit down beside me."

"I have to find my clothes, I have to get dressed."

I make my voice stern as I order her: "Jane, come here."

She flinches a bit at my tone and hunches her shoulders but she reluctantly walks over. I tell her to sit down and she chooses a spot a foot or so away from me.

"Closer," I command. She sighs and slides near.

"Your skin is awfully pink and it looks scrubbed, did you have a very hot shower?"

She doesn't say anything but she does nod her head once. I reach over and tilt up her chin, forcing her to face me but she refuses to meet my eyes.

"You feel naughty, don't you? But it's not a fun, sexy naughty, no, you're feeling like you're a sick, bad girl, right?"

Now she does meet my gaze and her expression is so sad, so unhappy, but she doesn't speak. Instead she presses her lips tightly together.

"You feel dirty, right? Like a dirty little slut?"

I hear both Brent and Harry protesting but Jane and I ignore them. We're on the same wavelength and I'm speaking directly to her emotions, her very negative emotions.

"Well, I'm a psychologist, Jane, so I know a few things about feelings. But more importantly right now is that I'm also a teacher who knows a lot about discipline. You won't feel better until we've satisfied your need to be punished for what you've been doing here."

The guys immediately start arguing with me but I've spotted how Jane's eyes widen at my understanding so I pull her across my knee, yank up the towel, and telling her she's earned six of the best – although God knows where I pulled that outdated phrase from – I smack her bare bottom hard. Very hard.

My hand-print shows pinkly on her quivering flesh. I figure she'll only last for one more spank and I'm right, the desired result is achieved when Jane bursts into body-wracking sobs.

I quickly lift her onto my lap to be cuddled tightly against my chest, and using soothing endearments like there, there my poor baby I tell her to cry it all out. I finger-dry her hair and play with the kiss curls around her face. All the while she sobs against my chest, her shoulders heaving.

Brent leans in close from one side and Harry wraps his arms around us from the other side of me so that the three of us are holding our girl safely cocooned in our joint embrace. We stay that way until Jane's tears resolve into a couple of hitched breaths and a hiccup.

She pulls away first and wiping her eyes tells us she's so sorry, she doesn't know what's come over her.

"No Jane, we're the ones who are sorry if we made you feel badly. We don't think you're dirty or bad, we would never think that way about you. To us you're wonderful, and this has been wonderful," says Brent.

"What we've shared here has been profoundly moving, Jane. I admit that all along I hoped we'd turn tonight into some kind of *special adventure* but this has gone beyond my imagination. Jane you are so very special to us," adds Harry.

I just give her a squeeze and kiss the top of her head.

"You guys are so nice," she whispers, "but it really is time for me to go."

Brent takes hold of her upper arms, forcing her to look at him, when he tells her: "Jane, we've always known you're a good girl and after what's happened between us all here tonight now we know you're a very good girl. Our very good girl."

His words elicit a small smile.

Then Harry exclaims: "No, you can't leave yet – I owe you one." Referring to his super-quick performance when he had his turn inside her. He's right, she is owed some pleasuring.

Pushing her back on the bed he scoots down until his head rests between her thighs. Jane doesn't move. Harry gently pries her legs apart about six inches or so. The skill he used hours ago when bestowing expert kisses on her mouth is now expressed on her body's most delicate flesh.

I can see Jane fighting the urge to squirm but she can't prevent a groan and then a gasp from escaping her lips. Watching her writhe under Harry's ministrations is so hot.

Brent and I take this as an invitation to lie down one on each side of her. I pull open the towel and soon both of us are caressing her bare skin, teasing and tickling. It doesn't take long before Jane is squirming with joy. Our kisses on her face, tits, belly, and thighs have her delightedly basking in our admiration and attention.

With loud sounds of enjoyment Harry continues tonguing her engorged clit, his fingers spreading her wetness up and down her slit until she reaches climax. While she's holding herself rigid Harry moves up and inside her. When Jane's legs stop trembling he slowly and tenderly makes love to her. Jane says her heart is full. Brent and I smile down on our girl.

Afterwards, in a post-coital embrace Harry insists: "Jane, you have to spend the night with us."

"Oh, I couldn't do that."

"Why not? Tomorrow's Sunday and there's no school or work. Well, actually I do have to go in to the clinic to check on a few patients and write up case-notes but that will just be for a couple of hours," said Harry, "I'll be sure to hurry back."

"No, I can't stay, I have to go home, otherwise Livy will worry wondering what happened to me."

"Ah, Olivia. Where did you tell her you were going tonight?"

"I said I sort of had a date."

"Huh, I like that!" exclaims Harry, "I thought we were having a REAL date."

"Well, I didn't know what was what, exactly, and I didn't want to say too much to Livy although you'd think she could keep one of my secrets since I keep enough of hers."

Each of us men exchange glances over Jane's head. We continue our work to persuade her to stay over saying she can call Olivia or better yet, send her a text.

Jane

It is really late and I'm so relaxed that I do feel comfortable enough to stay. I don't know what my craziness in the shower was all about but I'm past it now. However, I can't imagine that we'll ever have a night like tonight again so I guess I should make the most of it.

"You've convinced me," I answer adding: "I just need to send that text to Livy so she doesn't worry. She might not even be home but if she's out I don't want to say too much in case she shares it with whoever is around." I know my phone is somewhere under all the plates and food containers stacked up on the coffee table. Locating it I send a message to Livy:

staying the nite, ttyl

Olivia's reply comes back almost immediately. It's filled with emojis of question marks, exclamation points, red lips, hearts, "Congrats", and a huge thumbs up. The text reads:

I want details, details, details, and pictures !!!!

Livy always texts using full spelling and proper grammar. Everything she does is with one eye to the future and the scrutiny she'll face when her star rockets. Although she knows I could never be persuaded to share her private texts with anyone Olivia thinks it's wise to maintain her habits by always keeping in practice.

Leaning over my shoulder Drew reads the message and chuckles saying: "Pictures! What a great idea."

"NO WAY!" I cry out.

Brent laughs saying: "Oh yes, we have to have a photo but–" he puts up his hand to stop me from interrupting, "We'll have it tomorrow morning at Denny's when we're all fully dressed and sitting round a table with platters of breakfast in front of us. Otherwise she'll never believe you, will she?"

"I have no intention of telling her about... this," I wave my hand around encompassing the three men and the sofa-bed.

"Of course you'll tell," states Drew.

"We want you to tell her," adds Harry.

I look from one to the other and with a sinking feeling in the pit of my stomach realize I was simply the bait to be used to lure in Livy, the prize catch.

Ridiculously I feel tears come to my eyes but I furiously blink them away. No way am I going to let on that I thought this was something more. It wasn't, it isn't. It's all been just another move in their game to score with Olivia. I should be used to this sort of thing, well not quite this sort of thing, but...

"Jane, what crazy thoughts are going through your head right now?" asks Drew with a probing look.

"Oh, they're not crazy. I'm a realist most of the time who just enjoys little flights of fancy now and then, but I've definitely got both feet back on the ground."

"Stop that."

I look away because my eyes are glazed with unshed tears. I can't let the hurt show. If we all drop the subject right now I can stay inside the fantasy of being wanted and desired for myself but if I had to face facts, well... then I'll humiliate myself by crying.

"Oh Jane, we really thought that tonight would have instilled a little bit of self-confidence in you. God knows you've got plenty of reason to be proud and self-assured, you know."

"Really? You're trying to tell me that if Olivia was here right now that you'd even notice I was in the same room?"

"Damn, Jane, how can we explain so you'll understand?"

"Let me try," puts in Brent. He pushes me back down on the bed and bends over me so that his mesmerizing blue-eyed stare is concentrated on my face. As usual I'm drawn into his gaze and listen patiently while he speaks. I'm in no rush, I feel like I could stay locked in a trance with him forever.

"Each of us would love to have Olivia in our bed but so what? You've got to stop comparing yourself to her. No, forget that. Let's compare you to Olivia and then maybe you'll get it.

Olivia is much taller so her legs are way longer than yours but just look at how shapely your legs are! And your body is definitely curvier while Olivia has a more athletic build. You both have very pretty faces although you hide yours behind your hair too much.

The main difference between you and Olivia is that when the two of you walk into a room you hang back while Olivia takes center stage. She has a vibrant personality and her conversation and behavior demand attention but that's her thing, it's not your thing. What she has isn't better than what you have, but what she does is take her share of the limelight and more!"

"I can't compete with her."

"And you shouldn't try. Sure, most people – most men – will be dazzled by Olivia's performance but don't kid yourself that nobody sees you."

"There's such a thing as facing up to the truth, no matter how hard that might be," I answer.

"How can I convince you?"

"What about the fact that you've been arousing all three of us for hours?" interjects Harry.

"That's right! Isn't that proof that we all find you alluring, attractive, adorable..." adds Drew.

"Sexy and sensuous and soft and sweet," finishes Brent.

I looked from one face to the next and they seem to be sincere but I teeter on the edge of belief because I don't want to be fooled or to make a fool out of myself.

Drew asks: "Do you believe us?"

I look away for a moment then turn back to him saying: "I'd like to, I'd really, really like to."

They fall on me with questing fingers and fondling hands and eager lips and suddenly we are a whirlwind of naked flesh caressing and pressing each other for heated, passionate pleasure and I forget all about Olivia for a while.

Brent

I hope my words have gotten through to Jane. When she came out of the shower looking so sad and dejected my heart just ached for her. It made me question everything we'd been doing tonight.

I was so happy when I came home and found her primed just as Harry promised, well to be fair he said he only promised about 85%.

Even though Olivia has always been the main attraction for us – and pretty much everybody else, I have to say – the truth is I always notice Jane, even when she draws back into the shadows. It was wonderful to see her lying there with her lovely face looking up at me.

Her eyes are a light blue but they darken to gray the longer we stare at each other. She has this shy smile and an air of innocence that is so appealing. Earlier, I could feel her body trembling slightly as I untied her blouse and I just felt so protective of her. When she bit her bottom lip in concern it drove me crazy.

Now we're playing with her once again and she's smiling, giggling even, so that should reassure me that she's okay with everything.

I thought Drew's punishment solution was too harsh, especially with what we know about him being a disciplinarian and all. The three of us have talked a lot about relationships and sex over the years and learned how he has this leaning towards the kinky, but it seems to have been the right thing to do. Jane managed to move past the anguish she was feeling.

I can't shake this feeling of unease, though. I know it's because that phrase from my job keeps repeating in my head: *consent must be explicitly given, silence does not mean yes.* I need to hear it from her.

"Jane, I was really concerned about you when you looked so sad."

She gives me her small smile saying: "I'm so sorry about that. I don't know what I was thinking and feeling. It was all very mixed up in my head and I reacted badly."

"Do you think what we've been doing is wrong?"

"In my head, yes, but in my body, no. I'm loving every caress. But... I've been brought up to be a modest girl who shouldn't be having this much fun. However, reconciling this is my problem, not yours."

"How do you feel in your heart?"

"Oh! Oh, I've been repressing any kind of heart feelings."

"Why?"

"Well, this is all very intimate and fantastic but it isn't love." She makes that last statement sound like a question.

"Of course it's love. We love you, I love you. It's not a Valentine's hearts-and-candy love but it's a very real feeling. Loving you, Jane, as well as loving your body, just multiplies my enjoyment in all of this."

"Oh Brent, that's so nice of you to say. I like to think I can just let myself feel whatever I feel and anything I do or say is okay because we've all got this wonderful connection between us."

"We do!" I say, and the other two agree. "But I still need to ask you, to be absolutely sure, are you okay with this? I mean, have you given us your consent? Did we take advantage or have you joined in willingly?"

"Of course you took advantage! You with your mesmerizing eyes, and," she turns towards Harry and strokes his well-developed biceps, "you with your beautifully muscular body, and you, Drew, with your smart way with words that totally seduced me.

So yes, you guys all had the advantage because what girl wouldn't fall prey to your multiple charms! But to answer your question about giving my consent, Brent: *Yes! Yes! Yes!*"

Harry

It's late now. We decide to have some drinks and figure we'd all better have the same thing so no one will have icky breath. My words and they all laugh when I say that, but it's true and they know what I mean. Beer breath can sometimes smell and taste like sour milk, unless you've been drinking beer yourself.

Doesn't matter though because Jane wants to stick to water and she's the only one any of us will be kissing. She's a great kisser, she's a great fuck, she's a great gal. I was so right to talk the guys into choosing her. It's been a fantastic night, and it's about to get even more interesting if we can worm Olivia's secrets out of Jane.

I'll try the humorous approach, I think, and using my best camp gay voice gush: "Soooo, Janey darling, dish."

"What?"

"Dish the dirt, spill the beans, tell us all."

"All about what?" "

You know, Sweetie. You mentioned the burden of having to keep Olivia's secrets and we want to know what they are."

"Ah, no. I was just thinking about this the other day when I realized I've been keeping her secrets since we were five-years-old and met in kindergarten."

"Aww, I bet you were cute little things."

"She was. Her mother put her hair in curlers every night and every day Livy had perfect ringlets that she wore with a ribbon that was the same color as her dress."

"What about you?"

"Me? My mother cut my bangs until they were high up on my forehead. I looked awful. And I had lots of freckles then, too."

"So, did you have naughty secrets as children?"

"No, we were mostly good. Livy's mother watched her like a hawk. No sugar, chocolate, or candy, and no soda or chocolate milk."

"That sounds harsh. Olivia must have rebelled at times?"

"Oh yes. Her parents, well actually just her mother, is a bit odd. Very competitive. For example, both Livy and I had to have our height measured and marked on the door-frame of their kitchen. It really seemed to bother Mrs. Carstairs the one time when I shot up and was taller than Livy.

Livy was always thinner and when we reached adolescence I was quite chubby. I didn't slim down again until I was fifteen or sixteen. Of course being plump meant I filled out first and was wearing a bra at thirteen. Livy didn't need one but her mother got her one anyhow, a padded bra."

"Okay, that's a secret but not the kind we were thinking of."

"Well, I'm hardly going to give away a secret you can use to blackmail my best friend!" Jane laughs.

"Is there such a secret?" Drew asks quickly.

"Enough with the secrets. I'm not talking and that's that."

I straddle her and pinning her shoulders down drop my voice to a threatening whisper: "Ve haf vays off meking you talk."

Brent shakes his head at me complaining: "Are you supposed to be a Queen or a Nazi? Make up your mind."

"Maybe I'm a drag-queen Nazi, hmm? Or maybe... I'm *The Tickler*," and I proceed to attack Jane's tummy and sides.

She looks at me with a wry smile saying: "My super-power is that I'm not ticklish."

I sit back amazed: "For real? I've never met anybody who isn't ticklish."

"Aha, then that means all of you ARE ticklish!" she hollers and bounces around on the bed tickling first one then another of us. We're all ticklish, me especially. The roughhousing is fun and we end up in a tangle of limbs, gasping for breath. Except Jane, who is laughing at us.

"I think it's time to crash and since Jane is my date I get to take her into my bed for the rest of the night," I say, standing and pulling Jane up beside me.

She's wrapped the towel around herself again saying she really does need to find her clothes. I help her look and we do locate the three garments: halter-top, shorts, and panties. I take possession of her clothes, leaving her in the towel.

The bedrooms are upstairs in our narrow house so we head up, all of us carrying the remains of our dinner along with empty cans and bottles to drop off in the kitchen/dining-room combo on the next level. We dump the stuff in there, then continue to the top floor where there are two bedrooms, mine and Brent's, while Drew goes up to his room in what was originally the attic.

Brent pauses at the door to his room to issue a *welcome anytime* invitation, adding that he might end up joining us in the wee hours if he wakes up feeling lonely. We exchange good-nights and I head to the bathroom.

I'm delighted at winning custody of naked Jane but by time I get back to my bedroom she's deeply, soundly asleep. However, it's wonderful to spoon with her. Sometime in the early morning Brent climbs into the bed too and we all slumber on.

Chapter Four

Livy

I can't wait for Jane to get home so she can tell me all of her news. God I hope she doesn't spend the whole day with the guy, what if she stays over another night? No, she's back at school tomorrow because her practicum at the veterinary clinic finished up on Friday.

Maybe she met the guy there? I know she's not interested in any of her class-mates. Maybe he's a customer of the clinic – or another vet? What if she refuses to tell me?

No, she won't. Anyways if she tries to keep a secret I'll get it out of her. And if she gets stubborn I'll just ask Harry, he'll know who Jane was hanging around with.

Little Janey having a sleepover. On a first date, too. Oooh, I'm going to tease her about that, the naughty tramp.

Well, I can't just hang about all day. I've got to give myself a manicure and pedicure and shave every hair off my body, then finish with a deep-pore facial. Sunday is my grooming day and I find it very relaxing.

Ding!

Ah, a text and it's from Jane it's wait, it's just a photo it's... omigod. All three of the guys are having breakfast with Jane. So one of them was her date? Which one? No, that doesn't sound right. She must have run into them at the restaurant.

I'm going to text right back and say... no, I'm not. I've got to think this through. I don't have a clue what's actually happening and I'm feeling a little pissed off here, I mean the guys are kinda my property. I don't date them, but I know each of them is interested in me. And they're my friends, not Jane's.

Wait, am I actually jealous? of Jane? That's kind of shitty of me. Jane doesn't have anyone and she needs somebody. But why does it have to be one of *my* guys? If that's even the case. Hmm, I don't want to sound possessive or anything so I'm just not going to respond at all.

Jane

The waitress hands back Harry's phone and we all crowd round to see how the photo turned out. It looks great! We knew a selfie would be too much of a close-up with us all squashed together but this is a very flattering shot. Everyone is smiling and I'm grinning the most.

Harry forwards a copy of the picture to each of us. I don't bother writing a message, I just send the photo to Livy. I wish I could see her face when she sees it.

Waking up this morning, naked in bed with two men, I just lay there marveling over the fact that yesterday really did happen and it wasn't a dream. I would never in a million years have pictured myself in a polyamory relationship. And best of all I think it's going to continue, for a while anyhow.

I wonder if there were any other girls before me? Probably? but maybe not because it all feels very fresh and new and exciting.

I sneaked off to the bathroom and when I slipped back into bed I felt the men stirring. Pretending to be asleep I flung my hands over each of them, at groin level, and waited for them to awaken. We each enjoyed a bout of morning sex and then Drew arrived and I got serviced again!

We got to the restaurant early because Harry has to continue on to work for a few hours. Brent has some court prep to take care of so after we eat Drew is going to drive me home.

We ordered our meals and the food arrived on the usual huge platters. Coffee and orange juice, bacon and eggs, pancakes and sausage, hash-browns and toast. Lots and lots of food for four very hungry people.

I'm enjoying my pancakes but I'm listening for the message notification from Livy once she sees the picture. Nothing happens and I check the phone to see that the sound is on and it is. Maybe she's still sleeping? No, that doesn't seem likely, it's after ten already.

Livy always likes to have a lazy day on Sundays doing her beauty routines, which is something she really enjoys. She doesn't go anywhere without her phone oh... except the shower. That'll be it, she's showering and no doubt doing her complete shave. I'll hear from her as soon as she gets back to our room.

We've finished the meal and are all sitting back stuffed from the big feed. I can't believe Livy hasn't responded to my text. Is my life really so unimportant to her? Has she decided it's not worth the risk of chipping newly polished nails to reply to me? I've never stayed out all night before, she has to know that this was something special for me, so why is she being like this? She makes me feel so... so small and insignificant.

"So, I have a question for you guys," I announce. They look over at me and I continue: "Each of you has dated Olivia, right?"

They nod in agreement.

"But none of you have bedded her – also right?"

They look puzzled but nod again.

"Well that's because Livy is practically a virgin. She has had sex but that was years ago and I guess she didn't like it." Now I have their attention and their interest.

"It happened the summer we were fourteen. My birthday is in the Spring and Livy's is in July. Her parents had rented a cottage for a couple of weeks and rather than having a sullen adolescent on their hands they invited me along to keep Livy company."

"What, the figured two sulky teens was better than one?" quipped Drew.

"Ha-ha. We actually had a great time during the first week. Livy and I went for long walks where we talked non-stop the way young girls do. We were allowed to take out a canoe and paddle around the lake, and at night we lay on the dock looking up at like a million stars. There was almost no light pollution in cottage country back then. We decided we were very mystical and grown up.

As I say, the first week was great but the second week we met a boy. Actually, he'd been there all summer and had seen us arrive but he ignored us. His name was Paul and he was staying with his grandmother. One day when we were out in the canoe she waved us over to meet him and suggested the three of us go to the movies one night.

Livy's mother always kept an eye on us when we were out in the canoe so she knew we'd stopped to talk. When we told her what the old woman had said she agreed that we could go into town with Paul but not in a car with him. We could walk to the show and Mr. Carstairs would pick us up afterwards and drop Paul off on the way home.

I thought it was just a game Livy and I were playing at by competing for Paul's attention. It's true he was cute, and at sixteen he was old enough to be a conquest so we both used what minimal wiles we possessed. I filled out the top of my bathing suit so I made sure to flaunt the small amount of cleavage that I had. However Livy won by having sex with him.

She claimed it was her birthday present to herself, but the truth is she was that determined to win our competition. It was definitely her first time and probably his as well. They did it twice during that second week of our vacation and Livy told me she wasn't very impressed.

Paul, on the other hand, fell madly in love with her. Once we got back home he started coming by our high-school, and while Livy liked having an older guy from a different high-school drive up in a sports car – he had a Camaro, I think – he became a pest and finally she had to get her father to tell Paul not to phone or come around anymore. I know he wrote to her after that but I'm sure she didn't answer.

Of course Mrs. Carstairs thought it was all a hoot, and she boasted to her friends about Livy already turning the boys' heads. She wouldn't have been bragging if Livy had gotten pregnant, she would have been shocked and angry.

Anyhow, Livy told me that she wasn't going to bother with boys. She said she was glad she'd discovered this now so she could concentrate on her schooling and her career. She had already decided to become a famous actress and nothing and no one was going to stand in her way.

So, I'm pretty sure that Livy hasn't had sex in about ten years."

"Wow, that's quite a tale. No wonder she keeps it secret," comments Brent.

I immediately feel guilty for sharing too much information. I need to explain myself and say: "She's never told me it was a secret, we just talked about it way back when and dropped the subject after that."

"Yeah, but don't you realize that it means Livy is probably frigid?" states Harry.

"You can't make snap judgments like that," replies Drew in full psychologist mode.

"True, but she can't be a lesbian or she'd have made a pass at Jane."

"Not necessarily, but well, yeah Jane is irresistible so I see what you mean."

We all sit in silence contemplating the possibilities while I repeat the compliment of me being irresistible over and over in my head.

"Maybe she isn't actually frigid but just doesn't have a strong sex drive?" suggests Brent.

"No, that can't be right because she often mas..." I stop speaking and shut my mouth tight. Now I really have their interest but in the wrong way! They all lean in with eager, quizzical expressions.

"Stop it. I can't be having this kind of conversation about my best friend behind her back."

Harry gives a groan and tells me now I'm killing him with speculation. "I have this picture in my mind of the two of you in your beds in your dorm room in the dark... Dammit, Jane, how am I going to be able to concentrate on work now?"

"Hmm, now I've got that very same picture in my head too, thanks a lot, Harry!" complains Brent but he's laughing as he says it.

Catching Drew's eye I see that he's studying me and I feel like all my guilty secrets have been exposed. Then he smiles and I'm reassured.

The guys each toss some cash on the table and we all get up to go.

"I wonder if Livy is mad at you, Jane. Is that likely? I can't believe she didn't answer once she saw our picture."

"Maybe she hasn't seen it yet," I say but it's obvious to me and to them that I don't believe my words. "I can't imagine that she'd be mad, although who knows? Sometimes she tells me I'm very naive and she gets a bit overprotective."

"That sounds like something she learned from her mother," puts in Drew. We walk outside and head to the vehicles. After dropping Brent off at their house Drew continues to the school and my dorm.

"Thank you for bringing me home and I'm sorry to be taking you out of your way like this."

"It's no problem Jane, in fact I wanted to get you alone to have a little chat."

I look at him with a bit of trepidation. Drew is always the most serious and I wonder what he wants to tell me. God I hope he isn't going to analyze me over my behavior yesterday.

"I hope you don't feel that I was abusive towards you when I swatted your bum. I know it was shocking but I felt I needed to provide you with a cathartic release and tears are the most common form that takes. I truly believed you needed to have a good cry and being spanked gave you the excuse."

"Oh, I never thought anything of it, Drew. I was embarrassed actually because I did cry so hard and you were all being so nice about it. I just, well while I was in the shower I had a very strong emotional reaction to the situation. It left me feeling confused.

I mean is this a polyamory relationship? Or a one-night stand orgy? I wondered if I was simply duped like a stupid slut into putting out but even as I said those words in my head I knew that wasn't true. I felt nothing but kindness and consideration and even respect from the three of you. Yet something inside me said I was kidding myself and I was just a cheap whore."

"And that's why you felt you should be punished. Hmm, well if you ever want to explore discipline and submissiveness I'm happy to oblige."

"What?" I turn to look at him and no doubt my eyes are wide with surprise.

"Yes," he replies, smiling at me. "Not punishment but foreplay. Not physical pain but emotional and psychological triggers resulting in physical arousal and pleasure. Although a session across the knee is bound to smart after awhile because the smacks do sting."

"Okay, now I'm really confused. Are you offering to give me a spanking?"

"Would you like one?"

My mouth drops open and he chuckles saying: "Don't answer that, let me explain.

First of all this is just a take-it-or-leave-it offer with no strings attached. I would enjoy giving you a light spanking as a prelude to sex. And I think you would enjoy it as well. It isn't the actual spanking that's a turn-on but the dynamic of you bare and helpless, and of me dominating you; of you squealing and squirming, and of me enjoying the spectacle.

I think it would lead to a very rewarding sexual experience for both of us. I guess that sounds kind of dry... but I do believe it. Especially since I know it's a very popular sexual fantasy for many women."

I just sit there tongue-tied and blushing.

"Anyhow, I'll tell the guys that we had this conversation so that if you ever indicate you want to go up to my room then everyone will know what's going on, and that this activity truly is a private one."

"I don't know what to say..."

"You don't have to say anything, Jane."

"Yes, but I don't want to give you the impression that I want to do this. I'm not saying I hate the idea but I'm also not saying that I will do it." I trail off feeling my indecisiveness is immature and ridiculous.

Drew glances over at me and gives me a slow, crooked smile. I feel a tingling sensation go right through me. I think my face has turned even redder and I look away so my expression doesn't reveal how aroused I am by this conversation.

"Jane, the guys and I have all spent lots of time discussing our sexual thoughts and desires. Exploring the D/s realm is my kink; Harry is keen to bed two girls at the same time – girls who will also play with each other under his direction; and Brent just likes straight sex – no pun intended! By that I mean he says he doesn't see the point in sexy lingerie when a naked body is perfect, or role-playing when plain old-fashioned sex – and lots of it – is the greatest."

We arrive at the university shortly afterwards. Drew has certainly given me a lot to think about. In fact, I need to study and analyze the whole experience so I can understand my role in it.

Drew tells me he and the other two are interested to hear about Olivia's reaction to the photo and to our group adventure. *Me too!* I think to myself.

"I hope you'll let us know and satisfy our curiosity."

I lean over to give him a quick kiss and promise I'll be in touch. He makes a move as if to kiss me again, deeply this time, but that would be indiscreet in the school's housing complex.

The Girls

As grad students the girls got a good-sized room. They like living on-campus and both feel that sticking to the rules and routines of dorm living suits them best right now. The room is kept tidy but it's obvious which side belongs to which one of them.

Everyone is certain that Olivia Carstairs will have her name in lights one day. She's got the looks, the talent, and the drive.

Jane Hargreaves is a different type altogether but people believe her future success is assured as well. She has all the qualities that will make her a great veterinarian, and she's a personable and amiable young woman.

Jane's calm, clever composure is the perfect complement to Olivia's dramatic, in-the-limelight flamboyance. Their friendship is as tight as can be and, despite many attempts through the years, no one has ever managed to come between them.

Ambitious followers have tried to get close to Olivia in the hopes of sharing her spotlight, and bitter complainers have tried to poison Jane's mind against her bestie. But their friendship has endured.

People have often speculated what would happen once sex and love caught one of the girl's attention, but no one was taking bets on Jane being the one to fall first.

Livy

The moment Jane steps through the door I drag her over to sit down. On her bed, since mine is covered with different outfits I'm putting together for the week.

Grabbing her arm I stare straight into her face and say: "It's like twelve noon, where have you been? I've been going mental waiting for you to get home to tell me what's going on. Tell me everything that happened. I want to hear every detail."

"Did you get my text?"

"I got a photo that told me absolutely nothing – except that you were having breakfast with the guys. So how did that come about? No, wait start with when you got asked out on your sort of a date on Friday afternoon. Who asked you? And did it just happen on Friday? or have you been keeping secrets from me?"

"You know I can't keep anything from you."

"Good, tell me all. I've been dying to hear all about your sleepover."

"First, I have to say I'm pissed off at you for not answering when I texted you that photo. I kept waiting to hear from you but nothing!"

"I couldn't reply while you were with the guys. Omigod you're doing this on purpose to delay! Just tell me, tell me, tell me. You've been having sex, right?"

Jane nods with a happy but somewhat guilty look. She was with one of my guys! " Which one did you do it with?"

"All of them."

It's a rare occasion when Jane can make me speechless but with that bombshell I am rendered mute. I can only imagine the silly expression on my face. I probably look like a fish with my mouth open and my eyes wide and blinking while trying to process this news.

I finally manage to squeak out: "All of them? Really?"

Jane leans back with a shit-eating grin answering: "Yup, really. All of them, repeatedly."

"WHAT?" I know I'm shrieking but I can't control myself. I feel torn, I can't decide whether to take her by the shoulders and shake her or embrace her like a champion.

How could Jane of all people have had such an adventure? Why wasn't it me? Wait a minute, did I just think I wanted to be in Jane's position? Oh no, that's making me think of the variety of positions that *repeatedly* might mean, and imagining myself in them. Damn. Damn. Damn.

"Jane, I'm absolutely gob-smacked, shocked, blown away, astonished.."

"And? Are you also happy for me?"

"Jane, I don't know. I can't wrap my head around this. I mean, if you had said it was any ONE of the three guys I'd be delighted but ALL of them? That's just..."

I don't finish, I simply shake my head. I'm not sure what I'm feeling so I can't find the words to describe it.

Jane

Wow, I don't think I've had the upper-hand over Livy since we were in Grade Seven and I beat her in every race at that year's Sports Day. It's a sweet, sweet feeling.

"Okay but if you want to hear you can't keep interrupting. Here's the story:

You know I was doing a work-placement at the Small Animal Clinic where Harry works, right? Well, on Friday we were in the lunch area talking about movies and he said he'd bought that latest action film that I wanted to see and he invited me over to watch it. He's got a projector screen and said he'd make popcorn so it would be like going to the show.

When I hesitated because, well, you know how I am, he said it was fine because my practicum was over so no conflicts there. Of course that wasn't why I hesitated, I mean I hadn't even thought of that..."

Livy is making a circular hand gesture signaling me to hurry up. I know she's impatient for me to get to the good stuff.

"Anyhow, he has the weekend duty for the recovering pets that are boarding there so we agreed that I'd go to his house about four in the afternoon, not driving because parking is awful round his place, and if we felt like it we'd go out for a bite to eat afterwards. The movie is almost three hours long so we would finish up about seven or so.

I Ubered over there and we watched..."

"Wait," interrupts Livy, "is that what you wore?"

I look down at my halter and shorts, the outfit looking a bit rumpled after almost 24 hours and nod.

"Right, now I get why you said it wasn't a real date."

I roll my eyes at her snarky tone, continuing: "I told Harry that I said that and he pretended to be offended saying as far as he was concerned it most definitely was a real date."

"Oh, just go on with the story. You're at his place. Wait, what's it like?"

"Not your typical bachelor pad, that's for sure. The three of them bought this house on Riverside Drive a few years back, well it would have to have been since no one can afford a home there these days. I

t's one of the old skinny buildings and it's got so much character. Inside the door-frames are some dark wood, the door handles are those crystal knobs, the floors are all polished hardwood, and there's lots of built-in bookshelves and cupboards and stuff. It's gorgeous."

"I've only seen those places from the outside. The location is prime."

"Yeah, they got lucky."

Livy snorts at my comment saying: "Apparently you did too."

I start to giggle and she smiles for the first time since I got home.

"So, did you watch your stupid movie or did you start fooling around right away?"

"Of course we watched the movie, that's why I went there. We watched the movie and ate popcorn. Harry had a couple of beers but I only drank water, from a bottle that I opened myself, I'm not stupid." "Who all was there for the movie?"

"Just the two of us, the other two came home later on. So the movie finished but we weren't hungry yet so we talked about the film and the other pictures in that series and I didn't even realize that he'd put his arm around my shoulders. Next thing I know we're kissing and okay I haven't kissed a million guys or anything but even I can say that Harry's definitely got mad skills."

Olivia holds up her hand to stop me while she thinks for a moment before nodding in agreement.

"What a great kisser he is!" I enthuse. "And you know, the first kiss is always special, isn't it?"

Livy just gives me a look, she obviously doesn't think the same way.

"So we're having this fantastic kissing session – nothing else – but then he starts running his hands up my neck and through my hair like this." I sit forward and demonstrate. "It gave me the most delicious shivers and I can feel them again now.

While his hands were at the back of my neck he undid these buttons so the top of my halter came undone but it didn't fall down or anything."

"Show me," Livy demands.

I reach up to undo the buttons and the fabric falls just below my collarbone.

"Then he cuddles me, my back against his chest, and I'm waiting to feel his hands start creeping up my front but he never did that. Instead, he started licking and nibbling at my ear. So now he's really giving me shivers and goosebumps.

I was so distracted I didn't even realize that Brent had come in the room until he was beside me, sitting on the couch. I was kind of reclined back and he was at my hip level I guess." I pose myself against the wall and indicate where Brent was sitting.

"Then Brent, not Harry, but Brent untied my top and it fell right open. Of course I'm not wearing a bra because it's a halter-top so I'm bare-chested with Brent staring and Harry looking down over my shoulder."

Livy unties the bow and we both see how the top falls back showing everything.

"You were like this with Harry and Brent." I can't read the look in her eyes or the expression on her face.

Looking down I notice my nipples are hard so I stand up and grabbing a t-shirt out of my dresser-drawer I cover up. "Yes. Then Brent started to fondle me and then Harry's hands joined in and I was about to stop them but Brent leaned in and kissed me deeply and wonderfully. When he finally pulled back all I could do was stare into his gorgeous blue eyes.

Meanwhile Harry, at least I think it was Harry, had unbuttoned my shorts but it was definitely Brent who pulled them and my panties off and tossed them aside.

Suddenly I'm totally naked, Brent has taken his shirt off and is pulling off his shorts when Drew comes in."

"Wait, you're naked but Harry is still dressed and Brent is half-dressed and the three of you are squashed together on a couch and Drew suddenly shows up?"

"With bucket chicken."

Livy just closes her eyes and shakes her head so I continue: "He said something about oh good, a floor-show and that he'd like to watch for a bit before joining us."

"Joining you... Drew."

"Well, yeah. Anyhooo, details get a bit hazy after that. The couch folded down so it was like a large square bed and Brent lay back pulling me on top of him. We had sex and I orgasmed, then Harry rolled me onto my back and we did it missionary style but that was over really quickly. Harry apologized for being so speedy but he made it up to me later. Then I'm being shifted again, on to my hands and knees this time, and Drew does me doggie-style and I cum again. So many times!"

Livy's still wearing her poker-face but I know her brain is processing everything I've said. It feels like she's watching a film of my activities in her mind.

"So while Drew's pounding you from behind Brent and Harry are going at it?"

"What? No! God no, nothing like that. The guys were all naked but they weren't touching each other in any kind of sexual way, they weren't kissing or anything. They only kissed me. All over." I smile but Livy's face is still impassive.

"While I was having sex with one the other two were fondling and kissing my body, my hair, my face... When Drew was pounding me as you so graciously put it, Brent was stroking my uh.. my clit."

"God you can't even say the words yet you had no trouble acting them out! I can just see you crawling around sucking dick then moving on to service the next guy..."

"HEY! Can you hear yourself? Jeez, Livy why are you speaking to me this way? I don't appreciate it. You asked what happened and I'm telling you. You can't turn it into something else, something cheap and nasty, because it wasn't that way. I wasn't being used to service them, I was the one being serviced."

"Oh Jane, you're such a naive little fool. We'd better get over to the pharmacy and get you Plan B or whatever morning-after pill they carry, I know you aren't on any sort of birth-control."

"I don't need to go, the guys all wore condoms."

"Condoms, really? They all just happened to have condoms in the pocket of their shorts? My God Jane, think about it. Obviously this whole... thing was planned well in advance and you were just the right idiot to be tricked into playing along."

"You know I felt bad for a bit because yeah, when you stand back and look at what happened me and three guys wow, slut-city or what? But that's not how it felt to me or to them. In fact they all reassured me over and over that this was a loving adventure for them so you're wrong, Livy. Really wrong."

Livy takes my hands in hers and asks if it was a loving adventure for me as well. I say yes and she tells me she's glad but I can see she doesn't believe me. Plus, she seems angry. I think her anger is at the guys but some of it might be directed at me, too.

She wanted to know what happened and I told her but now I think she might be jealous. Putting me down and making fun of me is only to make herself feel better. Well, to hell with her and her insinuations. I've always supported her and kept her secrets but now I'm mad, too.

Next time Miss Kitty is performing I'm going to take the guys to see her show. I won't tell them until afterwards that they've been watching Miss Olivia Carstairs getting down and dirty. Let's see how long Miss High-and-Mighty lasts on her pedestal after that!

Chapter Five

Livy

It's been almost a week since Jane's adventure. Well, the one I know about, that is. She's gone out at night - several times - but didn't tell me where she was going. Maybe it was just for a coffee, or a visit to the Library, but she probably went to see the guys again. Maybe even more than once. Relations between her and I have been strained and we're barely speaking to each other.

I know I offended her and I'm sorry about it but when I try to apologize she just freezes me out telling me *there's nothing to be sorry for.*

I can't stop thinking about her stories. For me all stories become screenplays that I can see acted out in my mind. I've always been good at visualization. Sometimes I lie in bed imagining that I'm the one on that couch being kissed and caressed and I get so turned on.

I've wanted a good fucking for years but the catch has always been involvement with a man. They can't just screw you and go, no they have to lay claim to you and call it a romance. It's like they don't want you to be the kind of girl who puts out unless she's in love. Spare me!

And then there's always the worry that at some far-off day in the future some fat, balding loser will come forward saying *oh yeah, I had her way back before she got famous* and you'll realize that omigod that's true! although back then you thought he was hot. But instead it's Jane who is having the no-strings-attached liaison that sounds ideal for me. It's exactly what *I* want and need. I trust the guys totally and know that even after I become a Hollywood star they'll always keep our affair a secret.

Damn, why wasn't I the one they chose? Well, that's obvious. I would never have agreed to a one-on-one date in a man's house, and there's no way I could ever have known about this other possibility. How did little Janey manage to stimulate such a plan? and such a response? How can I be jealous of *Jane*?

Drew

Jane called me up to tell me about Olivia's reaction and the things she said. I passed it on to Brent and Harry, saying this is exactly what I would expect from Olivia Carstairs.

Because we've so often been at her beck-and-call when she needs an escort, or even just a ride somewhere, she's begun to think we're her private property. She's out-and-out jealous and resentful of our attentions to Jane.

Brent suggested that Jane might be feeling down because of this and we should invite her over to cheer her up. Harry readily agreed, as did I. We've planned a special evening just for Jane to reassure her that there's no truth to Olivia's mean comments.

Brent is in charge of planning the evening because as he said he's the most romantic of the three of us. It's true, I have other inclinations, and Harry is just a horndog.

Jane

I was so relieved to get Brent's phone call last night. Even though I knew Livy was just being spiteful and mean the things she said to me did stick in my mind. I was afraid I wouldn't hear from the guys again.

Actually, *afraid* isn't the right word. I mean, if our time together was to become just a wonderful memory then so be it, I never really expected anything more. No, what I was afraid of was that Livy's cheap shots would taint that memory.

Her words left me with a very clear picture of the men laying back in their chairs – maybe concentrating on the TV – while I scurried on hands and knees from one to the other giving blow-jobs. That was so far from the truth.

Of course I had performed oral sex on them but it was nothing like how she suggested. I made the choice to use my lips and tongue and fingers to tease them back into action and every groan my caresses elicited excited me. I was not treated like some cheap little bitch.

Anyhow, I'm going to their house tonight for another fun evening. Brent says it will be a *special adventure* so I wonder what he has in mind? Not sure how I'm supposed to concentrate in class right now while thinking about what's in store for me in just a few short hours.

Drew will wait for me in the staff parking-lot and drive me over. I'm really looking forward to it.

Livy

I can't stop thinking about Jane and the guys. Now I wish she hadn't told me. In fact I wish none of it had ever happened and that Jane was still my ally in everything and that she wasn't getting laid. That's mean, I know, but sorry, not sorry.

I wonder though... I expect she's told the guys all about telling me and my reaction. They're probably all thinking I'm a real bitch for trying to make Jane feel bad. Suddenly *Little Janey* is the heroine of the story but it's MY story and they are MY guys. They asked me out first.

Now I do sound like a nasty bitch with a real dog-in-the-manger attitude. This sucks, big time, but what can I do about it? It would be totally wrong of me to try to muscle in to replace Jane in her secret fling. Even though I'm like 100 percent sure I could. But maybe replacing her isn't necessary? Maybe, we could both participate?

It wouldn't be the same experience Jane had, of being Queen Bee to the three of them, but it could still be fantastic.

Although, I guess I would get the lion's share of the attention and that might make Jane jealous. Would she really object to me joining in? I can't ask her, what if she said *yeah it would be a problem*. Can I think of a way to hint about it? I'd love to have her suggest it to me. That would be perfect. Unfortunately right now I can't even get the time of day out of her.

Well, let's imagine this is a role and my character has to deal with this, how would I act that out to get the audience on my side? Should I just tell one or more of the guys that I know what happened and I want to play too?

I'm absolutely positive Harry would set it up right away. But I have no excuse to see Harry. Same with Brent, but Drew... hmm. That'll be tough 'cause he's such a smart guy but even the smartest men can be led by their dicks.

Now, do we do this with or without Jane? I guess it's their choice.

But I don't want to hurt her, I really do love Jane. I'm just torn right now between making something happen or waiting for somebody to issue an invitation. I'm not good at waiting.

This compulsion to get naked with these men and play all night long has become such a distraction. It's practically the only thing I think about.

Good thing Miss Kitty's got a show booking tomorrow night. I'd normally wait at least at least a week longer before making another appearance but I need some release.

And the lucky audience is going to get a magnificent performance. My ego desperately needs a major boost.

Harry

I was disappointed when I heard how Olivia treated Jane. I was really hoping she'd find the idea intriguing and would want to join us. Two women at the same time is my fantasy.

I can picture the scene with me telling Jane to undress Olivia and then, when she's stripped bare having her undress Jane. And of course all the while I'm giving instructions like *Jane, rub Olivia's nipples till I tell you stop* and *Olivia, using both hands squeeze and massage Jane's ass.* It would be great!

Now, are Drew and Brent in this fantasy too? Hmm, I'll have to think about that for a bit. We've talked about this stuff before and it was always understood that Drew would play his domination games privately so I guess I could act out my threesome fantasy on my own. Of course we'd join the other guys after an hour or two *or more!*

Ahhh, a few hours of having those two women minister to all my wants and desires. God, I can't believe I just got myself this horny while I'm at work. Now I've got to wait until this evening when I can take the pressure off with Jane.

Jane

Drew was leaning against his car with his arms crossed over his chest and looking very stern. It gave me a tingling feeling. I'm pretty sure that at some point, not tonight but some time, I will suggest we go upstairs to his room. Knowing what awaits me there makes me *sick to my pants*.

Livy might think I can't say the words out loud but I can and I will. Thinking about the things Drew will do to me makes me wet and the anticipation is just so arousing that I feel a throbbing deep in my vagina, my *pussy*, so there!

I hope he can't read these thoughts on my face.

I say: "Sorry I'm late, I hope you haven't been waiting long."

I hope he can't read these thoughts on my face.

"I shouldn't have been kept waiting at all, Miss Hargreaves. However, I've been told that tonight is your special night so you're forgiven. But if it happens again you will be properly punished."

That makes me squirm! But I hide it – I hope – asking: "My special night? That sounds intriguing."

"Brent has planned the whole evening around you, apparently. I'm sure you'll find it all delightful, as will we."

I just love his fussy way of speaking when he's using his disciplinarian voice.

We're driving just ahead of the rush-hour traffic and soon arrive at their Riverside home. Drew pulls into the driveway behind Harry's car which I recognize from the veterinary clinic.

I don't know what Brent drives or if he even has a car. Since he works downtown at the Courthouse it's probably easier for him to use public transportation.

As soon as I walk through the door Brent is there to kiss me and hand me a glass of champagne.

Harry appears behind him saying "Drink that down, Jane. You'll get another glass after your shower."

I drink the flute of bubbly in three gulps, kick off my shoes and follow them down the hall.

I was told that tonight I would be treated like a Queen and that they were my Royal Attendants, giving me all their attention. I'm already giggling at their antics.

Drew explains that when the home's original bath fixtures had to be replaced they chose to forego a tub and instead add a very large shower. Not quite large enough for four so I designate Harry to be the chief body-washer.

I'm made to stand with my arms extended while they remove my clothes. I purposely wore a t-shirt dress with bare legs for tonight's revels, so stripping me doesn't take long.

Once I'm naked Drew gets the shower running, Brent fetches an armful of fluffy towels, and Harry pours champagne over my breasts then licks it up, saying he'll be sure to give me a thorough washing. He's a sight to behold with the water running down his well-muscled chest and arms.

The rest of the night is a bit of a blur since I continue to drink champagne throughout our playtime. The bubbles make me chuckle and the wine makes me tipsy.

True to their word they do treat me like royalty, like a spoiled princess. Harry does the work of soaping every inch of me while Drew and Brent point out what spots he's missing except he didn't miss my chest like the two of them said so my breasts receive quite a bit of unnecessary washing... naturally I didn't object!

"Harry, bend her over so we can watch to make sure you give the Royal Asshole a good scrubbing," teases Brent.

"Oh! I thought that was Drew..." I murmur and after a surprised moment of silence am greeted with hoots of laughter.

"You're definitely going to feel my finger up your anus for that one, Jane!" threatens Drew with a wicked smile. "And I'll pop it in when you least expect it, too!"

I lean against the tiled wall and lifting up my leg order Harry to wash between my toes but he gets distracted by the view. Holding my foot against his chest he strokes my slit up and down with the washcloth, knuckling my clit each time, until I get distracted as well.

Then Harry drops to his knees pulling my leg up over his shoulder and attacks my pussy with his mouth. Literally! When he did this before he used the tip of his tongue to gently, almost delicately, vibrate and swirl my clit until I was in ecstasy. This time I feel a wide tongue loudly slurping the whole length of my slit before coming back to stab into my hole.

He's sucked my labia into his mouth and now his muscular tongue stretches inside me curving, seeking, and finding my g-spot. I shudder so hard when the white lights explode in my brain that my shaking legs give out. I fall on top of Harry and he laughs with delight.

"You gotta teach me that move, bro!" exclaims Brent just as Drew says "That was fucking hot!"

After rinsing me off Harry carries me out of the shower and all three men towel me vigorously until my skin is freshly pink. I get lots of manhandling, massaging, and caresses but I want... I want to screw!

They make me wait for it.

Harry scoops me up in his arms and easily carries me through to the sofa-bed. I don't recall the exact sequence of events after that but I did receive a lovely, lengthy back-rub. I lay on my stomach while lotion was kneaded into my skin by several hands, covering me from the tips of my toes to the nape of my neck, and leaving me sweetly scented.

"Where did you get this lotion?" asks Harry.

Brent replies: "From your bathroom, I don't have stuff like that."

"I thought it looked familiar but it's not meant for giving a body massage."

"I just saw the phrase *non-greasy formula* and I figured that was a good thing."

"Yeah, good point. Guys like you who are born good-looking don't need help like the rest of us. And it seems to be working but you should have asked because I have some stuff that's made specially for massages."

"That figures—"

"Mmmm," I interrupt with a groan.

"This seems to be doing the job just fine," Drew says in a dry tone.

Then delicious torments that last for ages are practiced on me. First, I'm partly shaved. Brent and Harry each hold a thigh because it's important that I keep still. Being pinned down, spread and helpless, works like an aphrodisiac.

Drew uses shaving cream and a safety razor to cut away the hair along the sides of my pubic mound. Then he very carefully trims back the curls that hide my clitoris exposing a gleam of wetness on that pink flesh. An extremely erotic exercise.

After that my breasts are kneaded, squeezed, suckled... then my belly and legs are massaged. They play my body like a musical instrument and I respond with a sweet soprano of *ooohs* and *aaahs*. At least that's how Drew describes it.

"Here, open this will you?" says Brent, tossing a small package to Drew. Brent has his hands full dusting me off with talcum powder.

"What is this thing?" asks Drew before reading aloud from the wrapper *The Bumblebee Vibrator*. That gets everyone's attention – *especially mine!*

It's a small plastic device painted to look like a bumblebee, and about the same size. While reading the instructions Drew tightens a velcro strap around his middle finger then, with the bee facing towards me he flips the on/off switch and the gizmo vibrates and buzzes.

Giving me that familiar wicked grin Drew applies the device without mercy to my newly exposed clit. Incredible, unbelievable sensations flood through my whole body. Of course each of them has to take a turn making me buck and writhe and beg for a cock to fill me.

"Jane!" they cry in unison.

"Such language," says Harry.

"Not at all ladylike," adds Brent.

"Definitely a cry for help," opines Drew.

They finally take pity on my over-aroused erogenous zones and declare that Brent, since he put it all together for tonight, would have the honors. He quickly enters me then complains that he might drown. The guys laugh and I join in despite my embarrassment because I'm desperately glad to get some completion and satisfaction at last.

Once I've been loved by each man we lie curled up together in a comfortable and happy heap of warm flesh. Harry asks Brent where on earth he found *The Bumblebee*.

"Some sex shop downtown."

That answer certainly surprises the two men who exclaim: "You? In a sex shop?"

"No, of course not. I sent one of the paralegals."

"Seriously? What did you tell her?"

"That I was going to a bachelor party and needed a novelty gift for the groom to use on his bride but I specified that it couldn't be anything nasty because well, it was for his wife.

She brought back this Bumblebee thing and when I asked why buying it took almost two hours she was like *oh boss, I'd never heard of half the stuff they have in there so I had to take the chance to find out about it all.*

She started to tell me about the strangest objects but I was like *no Eliza, we can't have this kind of conversation at work, it's inappropriate, it could even be called sexual harassment.* I didn't know what she bought, that it was a kind of vibrator, just that she told me the sales-clerk said it would make a wonderful gift so I thanked her and that was that."

"Well, I think it was a great choice and Jane here just loves it, don't you hon?"

"Let's just say I have a love-hate relationship with it, Drew."

"I still can't get over you doing what you did, Brent. I mean, you're the super-straight guy when it comes to sex. No frills and nothing fancy. I never figured you'd come home with sex toy!"

"That's because I don't think there's any need for extras. Sex is simply the greatest, it doesn't need to be dressed up or down because it's perfect as is.

Tonight, though, is different. Tonight is all about making Jane know that she's loved and cherished. So I'm willing to venture out of my comfort zone to make it a special night just for her."

He proceeds to tell me that he and Harry had thought about making my body into a birthday cake – pointing out that I'm already in my birthday suit – by coating me with icing and whipped cream and strawberries and chocolate sauce and smearing everything into a swirl of sweetness that they'd eat off of me.

"But Drew threw cold water on that idea when he pointed out what a mess it would make," says Brent.

Harry joins in: "So I suggested we lay down some plastic sheeting but then Drew said the sight of that would probably make you run screaming out the door, thinking we were trying to murder you. So we had to shelve that idea altogether."

Drew explains: "If we had a bathtub it would be perfect. We'll keep it in mind because you never know, we may end up in a hotel room some time."

I squeeze Brent's hand and thank him, adding "Everything has been so wonderful, I really do feel like a pampered queen."

He squeezes back, saying: "You know, just because I'm only into intercourse doesn't mean I'm not interested in trying new positions."

"I don't think I know anything other than the ones we've already done."

"Well there is something called a *Reverse Cowgirl* and it means you get on top but turned to face my feet." "

Won't that be uncomfortable for you I mean, doesn't your, it, well... bend the other way?"

He grins saying: "There's only one way to find out."

"Oh, this is going to be entertaining, eh Drew?"

"Harry, pour me a drink. We'll toast them if they manage it."

"Stop that," I say. "How are we supposed to do this if you guys keep making us laugh?"

I scoot down until I can throw my left leg over Brent's hips and then stroke him with my wetness to assist entry. It's an awkward position but I want to give Brent his fantasy so I don't complain.

I find that if I stretch forward it's easier to accommodate him. And that way I can massage his balls. His groans of pleasure are so gratifying.

"It can't be much of a view," I joke.

"Are you kidding?" he exclaims. "I can see you sliding up and down my shaft and that's a fantastic sight. And your ass is round like a peach and when we're finished I really think I'm going to bite it."

I squeeze him hard inside and he explodes. Drew and Harry give us a standing ovation and Brent leans over to nip my bum before hugging me tight. We kiss for a long, long time.

It's getting late for a week-night and we all have obligations next morning so I hop off for a solitary shower – much quicker this way – and Drew says he'll be driving me home.

"My car's at the end of the driveway and my first class isn't until 11:00 so I can sleep in." He explains.

I kiss Harry and Brent good night and thank them both for giving me such a wonderful special night. Harry assures me that he's already looking forward to our next get-together.

Brent holds my face in his hands and staring into my eyes asks me: "You know you're loved just because you're you, right Jane? You know I... we, we all think you're very special because you are."

I have to blink rapidly to hold the tears at bay as I whisper *thank you!* and Brent gives me a lingering, loving kiss.

When I get buckled up in the car I lay my head back and close my eyes telling Drew that I had a wonderful time and I'm very happy but my bones feel like they're made of rubber.

"I'm glad you enjoyed yourself," he says. "It's terrific to see you so content and relaxed."

I smile in response but then feel myself dozing and cat-nap the rest of the way home.

It's a relief to let myself into a dark room, meaning no conversation with Livy. I strip out of my clothes and just leave them lying on the floor before tumbling into bed.

I sleep deeply and dreamlessly until Livy's alarm wakes me next morning.

Chapter Six

Drew

Olivia doesn't try to slip away from me after my late morning lecture, in fact she's made a point of waiting until everyone leaves before sashaying down the stairs.

"I understand you've been seeing a lot – and I really do mean a LOT – of Jane lately. She's very dear to me you know, so I want to make sure that you guys are treating her right."

"You can see for yourself, Olivia. Jane – and yes, she's great – came up with a crazy suggestion for all of us to have a night out. We're all going to go to, if you can believe it, a strip-tease show! Why don't you join us?"

"Male dancers or female?" she asks but in an offhanded way, I can tell she isn't really interested in my answer. Instead, I see the wheels turning in her head as she figures something out.

"The exotic dancers are female and the place is called *Girls Galore*. It's going to be fun, you should definitely come with us. Maybe the show will... inspire us?"

She gives me her usual cat-like smile saying: "Girls Galore, eh? I can't come with you but I will show up. I promise. If you see Jane before I do tell her I'm really, really looking forward to it."

As I watch her walk away I notice that one, her shapely butt fills out those blue jeans perfectly; and two, she's up to something. I don't know what it is *yet* but I'm going to enjoy finding out.

Jane

Miss Kitty truly outdid herself tonight. I've seen Livy's performance before but this time she really does an outstanding routine. The men in the audience went mental, the men who accompanied me are entranced and I'm miserable. L

ivy is so beautiful and sexy. On stage she acts out a promise of mind-blowing sex, skillful seduction, unending pleasure... she's everybody's fantasy girl.

When Drew passed on Livy's message I immediately recognized the hidden sub-text for me. She doesn't know whether or not I'll reveal her secret but she probably assumes that's what I'll do.

I still haven't decided.

Yes, I'm horribly jealous but I also feel defeated and resigned to it. I mean, I can't compete with her. That show we just watched was sex personified. Livy is a star, a goddess, a winner.

Before the show she was peeking out from behind the curtain at the back of the stage, looking around until she spotted us. She didn't wave but she knows I saw her.

Livy once told me the audience is just noises in the dark so this was her making a point of finding out where we were sitting beforehand. Then she aimed her performance directly at our table.

Is this her way of giving me the ultimate put-down? Is she signaling the men that she has all this to offer and she's available to them? Will she really cut me out?

We've been best friends for twenty years, from tots to teens to young adult women, and we've shared so much. Maybe she's letting us know that she wants to join in and be one of five in our special adventures?

I think she'd sideline me pretty quickly. Maybe not on purpose but just because of the way she is and how the men are attracted to her like moths to a flame. I know it will really hurt to see them all fawning over her and leaving me out in the cold.

I'm not going to tell them the secret that Miss Kitty is really Olivia Carstairs. I'll leave it up to her to make the next move.

Livy

I have no trouble finding them in the audience. The clientele is mostly made up of single men sitting on their own so a table of four is noticeable. They're not right up by the stage but their seats aren't too far back so they'll get a good view. And I'm going to give them plenty to look at.

Jane sees me but doesn't smile or wave. Has she revealed my secret identity to them? I think she must have, why else would she bring them here? Unless she's saving up the surprise until after my show?

Hmm, I think I'd like them to know now. They'll watch so intently if they know it's me who they're seeing stripped bare and teasing them. Damn, there's no way for me to know what she's told them... Well, I better make sure this is my greatest performance ever!

I want everybody to be electrified by this show, I'm counting on a great outcome.

Drew

Miss Kitty's show was the final performance, ending tonight's entertainment. The stage remains dark and most of the people in the audience get up to leave.

Since it's a week-night the live performances stop at a reasonably early hour. Probably dancers have babysitters waiting - or maybe some will hurry home to cram for tests at school?

There are no lap-dancers at this venue so the remaining clientele are there to drink. The bar will stay open for another few hours.

Brent signals the server for our tab. As the best-looking guy in the group he always gets great service. We're used to it by now. We stay to finish up our drinks and to discuss what we've seen.

Brent speaks first saying: "That was quite a show, eh? Jane, this was a great idea. That girl is a real performer. Beautiful and with a fantastic body, of course, but what moves and mannerisms! Her music was an inspired choice, too."

Next, Harry says: "I have to tell you guys, Olivia Carstairs is no longer my *numero uno* dream-girl, it's now Miss Kitty all the way!"

I've been watching Jane and notice she's very subdued. She's downed her drink, just a soft drink, and looks ready to leave right now. She senses me watching her and meets my eyes with a challenging look in hers.

I start to chuckle. "Jane, don't you think it's high time you told us Olivia's secret?"

"What do you mean?" ask Harry and Brent together.

Ignoring them I turn to her saying: "Will it feel less like a betrayal if I tell them?"

Jane starts to speak then stops for a deep breath before beginning again but at that moment all of our phones ding with new message notifications. The messages are from Olivia and each one is the same:

Looking forward to seeing more of you now that you've seen... what you've just seen.

"What's that supposed to mean?" asks Harry.

Jane sits up straight and speaks briskly: "It means *now that you've seen all of me* but Livy would never put that in writing."

Brent's mouth falls open in surprise but Harry is still trying to figure it out.

"Harry, Olivia is Miss Kitty." I tell him.

"WHAT? No, NO!! Really? Holy shit! No wonder I fell for her. Again!"

Brent turns back to the stage as if he can re-capture the show he just witnessed. I can see the memory of Olivia's routine, and his thoughts about it, chasing across his face. Jane is also watching Brent and her face is expressive.

"So that was Olivi–"

"Ssshhh. Keep your voice down. It's a secret, remember?"

"That's why she covers her hair and wears the cat-mask the whole time, so no one will know who she is," says Jane then turning to me asks: "How did you know?"

"Simple! Olivia has treated me to that sassy strut more times than I care to recall. After every lecture she walks away swaying her hips because she knows I'm watching. Tonight I recognized her when she pranced across the stage with that same proud, self-satisfied move. That's when I figured out that she knows we're here watching."

I look back at Jane but she shakes her head saying: "You told her, not me. As soon as you passed on her message I realized it. Remember? She told you to tell me she was *really, really looking forward to it*. She probably thought I'd already told you."

Harry suddenly bursts forth with a thought that has obviously been growing in his mind: "Hey, Olivia said she wants to see more of us and since we know Jane told her what happened then that must mean that she wants to join us! Oh, that's great, really great. The first thing I'm going to ask her to do is give us a private strip-tease show, and maybe a lap-dance, too. What do you think?"

Harry's enthusiasm makes me smile. I've interpreted Olivia's message the same way and it's a very, very interesting proposition. One I'm very much looking forward to.

Brent speaks quietly to Jane but I can hear him. "

Sweetie, you don't look too happy. Do you feel badly about Olivia's secret coming out? You shouldn't, it's not like we'll ever say anything to harm her. And it's really not fair for you to carry the burden of a secret this big. How long has it been going on?"

Jane gives a deep sigh before answering. "About two years... maybe a bit less. She started soon after she entered grad school because the money she makes stripping is really incredible. She told her parents that she's been doing some modeling. When her mother wanted to know which publications she improvised and said for art classes at the U.

The School of Art does pay very well. And Mrs Carstairs won't tell anyone because Life Drawing means nudity. Anyhow, Livy makes great money and she enjoys it. I couldn't do it though. I'm grateful my parents are rich and support me because the funding really isn't very much."

"Actually this shouldn't really be such a surprise," I remark. "We all know Olivia is a great actor and she loves being the center of attention so this is a natural fit for her. Great practice on how to engage the audience and you can see she just revels in the applause."

"So when can we all get together?" Harry is so eager.

I see Jane's shoulders slump and her mouth turn down but Brent gives her a squeeze and she pastes on a smile for him. I can't help but notice how her unhappiness shows in her body language but she speaks quite brightly when she answers.

"You guys figure something out and let us know. Right now, I've got to get going. Livy will be waiting for me, wondering what the result of our discussion is so... I tell her that we'll all be getting together soon, right?"

"You bet!"

"How does Olivia get home, and why didn't she wait for you?" I ask.

"She has a driver waiting for her to finish and he whisks her right away. She doesn't dare hang about in case somebody sees her face. I think she's overreacting but on the other hand some of these guys might get ideas."

"Jane, every single guy in this place tonight was given ideas!" replies Harry with a wolfish grin.

I drove us to the strip-club so we all leave together and I drop Jane off at her place before we three head homeward.

"I'm going to be thinking about Olivia all night now. And if I do manage to fall asleep I know I'll be dreaming about what we saw and what we're going to be doing. God, I hope it's soon," says Harry.

"Drew, did you think Jane looked a little... I don't know, not jealous or anything like that but sorta down, or something?"

"I did, Brent, and I think it might be an issue for her. Jane will always feel like plain Jane when Olivia is around and I'm betting she's felt like that since they were teenagers."

"Hey, Jane is great, right? But you've gotta admit she's no Olivia," puts in Harry.

"Thank God!" exclaims Brent. "I don't think we could handle two Olivias."

I made a mental note to get hold of Jane sometime tomorrow to discuss her thoughts and feelings about Olivia joining our special adventures. It's no use asking Brent to do it because she'll pretend everything is fine even if it isn't. Brent is a very black-and-white kind of guy who won't be able to catch her out in a lie.

Of course she'll lie to me too but I'll be able to see through the pretense.

Livy

No one responds to my text messages but I expected that. They'll want to discuss it. Omigod I'd dying to know what they're saying! Where is Jane? Aarrrgghh, she can't get home soon enough! I want her to hurry, hurry, hurry, because I need to know every single thing that everyone said.

Edwin can tell I'm anxious about something. He saw Bruno wink and heard him say I'd given an exceptional performance tonight.

I'm in the back of the limo and I can't sit still. Edwin remarks that I seem to have ants in my pants tonight and I burst out laughing. I think that's a pretty accurate description of what I was feeling then and still now even though I dealt with my immediate need in the shower.

It took me less than a minute to finish but I got all tingly again when I washed up. It's true when they say the most powerful erogenous zone is the brain because my thoughts have got me steamed up with desire.

Where the hell is Jane? I hoped she'd be back in our room by time I finished up in the bathroom.

When the door opens I practically pounce on her. It reminds me of when she finally came home after her first sleepover with the guys. Was that only a little over a week ago?

I'm trying to get a read on her but she's got her resting bitch face on. I desperately want to get my own way so I go on the attack accusing her of betraying me and our friendship by blabbing my secret.

That gets a reaction. She narrows her eyes at me saying: "You should never have burdened me with keeping your secret in the first place. If you think it's okay to be doing what you do then admit to it, don't hide."

"But you know why I hide, Jane. My career shouldn't have to suffer at some future date because I need to earn money now. We don't all get subsidized by our family, you know."

That's a bit of a low-blow because Jane pays the bulk of our bills so in fact I am being subsidized by family – her family.

"Anyways, I didn't tell them," she says adding, "Because Drew guessed. Well, from what he said it wasn't much of a guess, he recognized your sassy strut or whatever he called it."

"Did he really?" I discover that I like the idea. "But he wouldn't have figured it out if you hadn't taken them all down to the club in the first place."

Jane sighs saying, "No, you're right about that. I was angry with you–"

"I noticed, you wouldn't talk to me."

"I talked, I just didn't say much."

"The only thing you said was I'm *fine* and *everything's fine*, I wanted to shake you."

"Well you made me feel cheap after I'd had such a wonderful time and it felt like you were trying to ruin everything."

"Oh Jane I am sorry for that. Maybe I was a little jealous? But really I'm glad you had a great time, that's what I want too! Jane, please Janey, can't we move on from all that? I really, really, really want to experience one of your special adventures."

"You mean you want to be a cheap slut too?"

"Totally!"

"Well, you're in luck," she answers with a smile, "because the guys *totally* want you, too. However, there's just one thing and I don't know what you're going to think of this but first you have to have a private session with Drew."

I'm intrigued! But I keep my thoughts hidden stating: "Drew who's into some shady S & M stuff?"

"No, it's nothing extreme like that. It's just he says he has this thing about how arousing it is for a couple to play-act a dom and submissive role. He mentioned a *light spanking* as foreplay. He thinks you need to be humbled in order to fit into our dynamic."

I take a deep breath and think about what she's said. I have to show reluctance but deep down I know I've been sassing and bratting him at school because I want to test his limits. Inside I'm on fire at the thought of Drew disciplining me... or at least, trying to!

Jane

I'm really glad Livy and I have gotten past our sort-of-a-quarrel but if I'm honest I wish she wasn't going to join us in our special adventures. But she is and that's that. I'm tempted to bow out of the next get-together but sitting home thinking about the four of them will be way worse so I've just got to put a good face on things.

First, though I have to go into the bathroom so I can send a text to Drew:

told L yes but 1st a private sesh with u to humble she said ok hope ok with u 2

Drew's reply comes back right away:

i love you

I sure would like to be a fly on the wall of that bedroom to see Livy being dominated by Drew! but I know that the problem I'm facing isn't going to go away. With Livy and I in the same room all three men will gravitate towards her and that'll make me jealous but I can't let it show and I'm not sure how I'm going to manage that.

At different times in our lives Livy has been incredibly generous or else very possessive. I know she expects me to behave in a certain way and if I don't she acts like a favorite pet has suddenly taken a bite. I suppose

I have expectations of her too. It's something I've never really thought about before. I'm not a very introspective person, I have more of a *shit happens* attitude. A bit defeatist, I guess.

If I'm treated like an afterthought at our next get-together then I'll just make that my last special adventure. I'm not going to push myself forward. Livy does that but it works for her because she's always welcome. I'm not going to be pitied and I'm not going to give in to self-pity either. I also have a fair bit of *it is what it is* in my attitude.

And the fun-and-games we're having right now were never going to last forever. My long-range goals include an emotionally rewarding career, marriage, and family, and nothing's changed my mind about that.

I do hope we can continue our special arrangement for some time but I've already accepted that one day it will end and, with Livy joining in, that day might be sooner than I'd like but so be it.

Drew

Jane's text drove my libido into the stratosphere. Harry's got a major crush on Olivia but I've been head-over-heels for years. In the interests of striking while the iron is hot I'm going to text her right away with an appointment. Not a date, I might as well establish the ground rules from the start. In fact, I'll let her know that a session with me must follow certain rules. I'm getting hard just thinking about it.

I go downstairs to tell Brent and Harry that I need the place to myself tomorrow around supper hour, say from 5:00 until 7:00, no better make it 8:00.

Brent asks *what's up?* and I explain I'm going to see Olivia privately. Both of them know what that means, or rather what I'm hoping it will entail, and Brent gives me a thumbs-up while Harry gets a sour look on his face.

"Harry, you know you have to share. And besides, you want a lap-dance with Jane and Olivia crawling all over you. Hopefully I'll be able to tame Miss Kitty so that you can have your desires fulfilled."

Harry nods then turns to Brent suggesting the two of them take Jane out for dinner. "We can spend the whole time speculating about what's going on here."

"I don't think that's a good idea in a public restaurant, Harry. We're just going to get turned on and we can't go back to Jane's place because she's in residence. Maybe instead of dinner we should go to a show? That way we can't talk about it."

Brent gives me a serious look when he adds: "But you're definitely going tell us all about it afterwards, right?"

"No worries! I'm going to want to share, it will give me a chance to re-live it all over again."

"Damn Drew that means you get to have her first and after all these years of all of us trying Yeah, we're gonna need to hear every detail.

So, I'll pick up Jane right after I finish work and we'll meet you at the mall. I'm sure there'll be something playing in one of the theaters there that we all want to see."

"Great, thanks guys. Listen, I don't think you should bring Jane back here after the show. Things will be a little intense so I think we should plan on all of us getting together the following night."

"Sure, sounds good to me."

"Me too."

I leave them to go the kitchen for a coffee, caffeine never keeps me awake, and to compose a text to Olivia. I want to word it just right.

Livy

I don't get a text or a phone-call from Drew, I get a calendar appointment! The automated app asks me to confirm tomorrow at 5:00 pm, duration TBD, with an added note saying *Don't be tardy!*

Well, well, well. Of course I'll be fashionably late. I'm getting excited just thinking about him waiting, anticipating... He thinks he's going to have everything his own way but I have a strong will, too. Of course that's exactly what he's hoping to break. Silly man.

I wait almost half-an-hour before sending a confirmation. Doctor Professor Andrew Thomas doesn't have as much of an upper-hand as he imagines, I know the value of my powerful attractions.

Chapter Seven

Jane

I enjoyed going to the show with Brent and Harry. It's great to socialize with these guys, and it's nice to know that it isn't just about the sex every time they see me. Although the sex is really great, too!

That makes me think about the last time Drew and I spoke in person and I asked him how this thing we have going on should be classified.

"I'm not sure, Jane," he answers and I can see he hasn't considered the question before. "I think I would call it polyamory, which isn't a sexual orientation or at least it isn't yet... although, perhaps polyfidelity is a better description.

All of us are in a non-monogamous sexual relationship but it's a closed group. Well, other than opening the door to let Olivia in! But the point is we're only sexually active within our group."

"Even Harry?"

"Yes, and both Brent and I are surprised at that. He might have gotten bored soon - no reflection on you, it's just his nature - but not now that Olivia is joining us too."

I'm thinking about that conversation while we're sitting in the mall's Food Court having a snack. Despite having stuffed ourselves with junk food from the overpriced concession stand! Harry orders a meal from the Thai place saying he needs lots of protein and calories to maintain his bulk and I compliment him on the magnificence of his muscles. He really has an amazing physique and he's right to be proud of it.

Brent complains that he's feeling left out but we both laugh at him while pointing out the different women – and even girls – seated throughout the food court who are staring at him like he's on the menu. He truly is an astonishingly handsome man.

No doubt everyone is wondering what a girl like me is doing with a buff hunk and a male model.

I ordered a chocolate ice-cream sundae but keep stealing fries from Brent's plate. He slaps at my hand and says if I don't behave he'll turn me over to Drew to teach me a lesson I won't soon forget.

I fake a shiver of fear and whine back "Can't I just have one french fry?"

Then he tells me I can have as many as I like from my own order which he'll be happy to buy me so long as I stop taking his.

Of course I steal another fry but offer him a spoonful of soft ice-cream which he takes. Then he licks the spoon while staring at me with his amazing blue eyes. I'm pretty sure my mouth is just hanging open and I look like a complete idiot.

However, we do start wondering how things have gone with Drew and Livy. I tell the guys it's time they start calling her Livy too. Olivia Carstairs is the actor, Livy is our friend.

Drew

I'd have won a bet on Olivia showing up late. When she finally does arrive she throws me for a loop by what she's wearing.

She's dressed up as a private-school student from her braided hair to her saddle-shoes. White blouse, striped tie, plaid skirt, white ankle socks and, best of all, white waist-high panties although I don't realize that until later.

She told me afterwards that she'd borrowed the costume from one of the exotic dancers at Girls Galore. All I know is that it's a perfect fit and a perfect look for the play-acting I have planned. The naughty schoolgirl getting properly punished.

I can see by her smirk that she knows she's caught me by surprise. I'll make her pay for that – and for her tardiness – but first I acknowledge her uniform with applause.

Then, without saying a word, I usher her in and point the way upstairs. She makes sure to add sufficient swing to her walk to set her short skirt swaying. I'm given a delectable glimpse of white cotton panty on each stair.

By time we reach my rooms in the attic I've already played out several scenarios in my mind. Tonight will be the culmination of so many fantasies, daydreams, wet dreams, and imaginings.

Olivia strolls around my room with cheeky curiosity reading titles on my bookshelves, lifting up framed photos, touching ornaments, while I just fold my arms over my chest and wait in silence.

Finally she turns her attention to me and I demand: "What's your excuse for being late?"

She shrugs with indifference. "I was busy and lost track of the time, I guess," is her saucy reply.

"You're not exactly making a good impression, are you?"

Olivia comes right up close to me and in a breathy voice asks: "Oh Sir, are you saying I don't impress you?"

I raise an eyebrow in reply then tell her to unbutton and remove her blouse. She does so revealing that underneath she's wearing a white undershirt that emphasizes rather than hides her perfect breasts.

After a good look I say: "Take that off, too."

Now she's topless except for the narrow tie. I have plans for that tie. In the meantime I study her lovely tits and hard nipples.

It's so difficult not to reach out and caress but I deliberately hold back. Olivia's power lies in her ability to make men lust after her – me included – but now is the time for me to disarm her.

In the middle of the room I've placed a wooden chair, a sturdy Windsor with a wide, solid seat. I sit down and beckon her near.

She comes hesitantly at first then lifts up her chin and marches over. She clasps her hands behind her back thrusting her breasts forward in such a tempting manner.

Despite the nudity there's nothing coy about her. Is that because of her naked dancing? Or did she start performing because she enjoys being nude in public?

"Can you explain to me why you're here, Miss Carstairs?"

She swivels back and forth, a move that sets her breasts swaying, and in a sing-song voice says: "I'm a naughty girl who deserves to be thoroughly punished."

I sit in silence until she meets my gaze. "No," I say, "This isn't punishment, it's humiliation." And with that I pull her across my knee and flip up her pleated skirt. Wearing the full-coverage panties was an inspired choice. So delectable.

"A good, old-fashioned spanking is always performed on the bare bottom," I declare. "So, I want you to pull your panties down yourself and offer me your naked backside like a gift."

She tries to stifle the little gasp she gives but I hear it and smile with satisfaction.

"I don't want to," she whines in a subdued voice. I say nothing and after waiting a full minute she reluctantly reaches her hands to her waist and starts to peel down her underpants.

"Slowly," I instruct, and she slows down to reveal inch after inch of tantalizing pale pink flesh. Once she is fully bared I pull her panties down around her knees and unknot her necktie. Drawing her arms back I bind her wrists together so she can't try to cover herself with her hands. Then I unbuckle her skirt and toss it aside.

Grabbing hold of her braid I pull until her head lifts, and her torso with it so I can roughly fondle her tits.

Demonstrating each action as I speak the words I say: "Here I am grabbing your tits, slipping my fingers into your slit, and smacking your bare ass." The swat makes her flinch so I quickly deliver half-a-dozen more. "While you lie across my lap utterly helpless and exposed. You have no power to wield while your hands are tied and your body is stripped down to those bits that interest me."

I give her another half-dozen smacks.

"That doesn't hurt," she jeers, trying to show some bravado.

"It only has to hurt your pride and dignity and I'll bet it's doing that! It must feel incredibly silly to be in your position, but I have to confess I'm enjoying the spectacle of you squirming and squealing. Your round bottom is a lovely sight, so appetizing, so inviting."

She struggles to escape but I keep applying spanks, not too hard, to her shapely bum which is warming up to a rosy pink shade.

"I'm not interested in causing you pain, my dear, the whole point of this is foreplay. I take pleasure in mastering you. The threat of being soundly spanked to a fiery red is a wonderful fantasy but that's it. A real spanking like that would hurt and I never want to hurt you.

However, I do believe being disciplined like a naughty little girl will elicit a thoroughly aroused response at being mastered. And I certainly enjoy having you at my mercy.

You can't see my face but I expect you can hear the amusement in my voice, smiling at you squirming with shame and embarrassment. I really enjoy the way your fleshy butt jiggles with each smack. I'm loving this! and the length of this session depends entirely on you."

"What do you mean?" she gasps.

"You can put an end to this humiliation by simply thanking me for the lesson. I'll administer a couple of stinging slaps, you'll wiggle and cry out, and we'll be done."

She doesn't say a word so I continue with the light spanks, occasionally giving a loud contented sigh or a chuckle under my breath.

Finally, in a small voice, she utters the words I have ached to hear for such a long time: "Thank you for giving me this lesson."

I can't resist saying: "Pardon? You'll have to speak up."

In agitation she loudly calls out: "Thank you for teaching me a lesson, Drew. And I oblige by leaving my hand-print with two hard stinging spanks, one on each cheek. She does squeal and she does squirm and when I slide my hand to her snatch she's soaking.

I knew it! I think in triumph. *I knew she was the kind of girl who would be aroused by being dominated.*

I rub her ass with one hand and her tits with the other. Shifting to her slit I feel her quiver as I flutter my fingers until we can both hear her wetness. This is her comeuppance, this is the final exquisite humiliation.

I can't wait a minute longer. I yank the tie from her wrists then push her off my knees and onto the floor. I enter her in a rush but I try to be gentle. I haven't forgotten Jane revealing it's been ten years or so since Olivia had intercourse. I try, but holding back is impossible. I pound and squeeze and am gratified to feel her legs wrapping round me, pulling me in closer.

When I finish I cover her in kisses from tip to toe. There she lies on my bedroom carpet in all her naked glory. I can't stop touching her.

We get dizzy from kissing until we remember to come up for air. Then I turn her over and cover the back of her with more kisses and caresses. Lifting her hips I enter from behind, my favorite position - especially when I can admire my handiwork on a prettily reddened bottom. This time I last long enough to bring her to orgasm twice.

"I hate the thought of you ever getting on that stage again and letting strange men see your perfect body, and yet I just love the thought of them all wanting you while knowing that I'm the one who gets to have you."

She looks up into my face with an open, fresh, innocence. No smirking, no winks, no innuendo or insinuation. Just a woman responding to a man's adoration.

"I feel like a virgin," she confides, "because I'm so inexperienced. I'm really good at talking the talk but I've never felt anything like this."

We kiss deeply then I sigh saying, "Brent and Harry are both going to make love to you tomorrow night and I'm going to have to pretend I'm okay with that, and you know what? I will be, because you deserve the experience of a special adventure.

Jane told us how you don't want to commit to a relationship so I won't be possessive but at least for this one moment you are mine, mine, all mine."

She smiles up at me and confirms: "Yes, Drew. Tonight I'm all yours."

Brent

Being with Jane and Harry at the show tonight made me realize how much I enjoy her company. She's funny and smart and has a great body that she shares with such generosity.

I'm starting to have mixed feelings about tomorrow night. I mean, yes for the longest time I've wanted to have sex with Olivia – Livy – but I don't want Jane's feelings to be hurt and I think they might be.

Maybe it's all in my head but I see Jane as so tender and vulnerable. When I make love to her I really am in love with her but here I am in my room on my own and I'm still in love with her.

Will it bother her to see me enjoying sex with Livy? I really don't think she'll mind much so long as I then make love to her with equal enthusiasm.

Hmm, when I think of being with Livy it's sex – fucking – but with Jane it's making love.

Did seeing Livy's performance as Miss Kitty change the way I feel about her? Yes, it did. It made her seem like a larger-than-life sexy box-office bombshell. Somebody to enjoy watching but maybe best kept at arms-length.

If Livy were to cancel tomorrow night I'd be disappointed, but if Jane were to cancel I'd be devastated. Jane's definitely my preferred kind of girl, she's a lifetime proposition.

Jane

Livy's description of her session with Drew gets me all hot and bothered and I admit as much to her adding: "Some feminists we are!"

"I know!" she exclaims, delighted that we're on the same wave-length. "If anyone had ever told me that I would submit to that kind of treatment I'd just laugh in their face. As if I'd ever willingly give up my power! Yet I did.

Maybe that's what it's like for those top-level executives who go to a dominatrix. Maybe all of us who prize keeping ourselves in control do need some sort of release-valve to take the pressure off now and then."

"Okay now I have a confession to make," I say, certain my face is wearing a guilty look. "I faked that demand that you had to have a private session with Drew before you could join in on a special adventure. I have no idea why I did that. Well, except maybe because I was interested to find out exactly what he would do to you and what it would feel like. Sorry I lied about it to you, but Drew was thrilled I said it."

"I'll bet he was! I totally believed he said that. You're a sneaky little bitch, aren't you? If you want to know what it feels like to be spanked maybe I should spank you!"

"Oh ha-ha, very funny. No, seriously now. It sounds like you were really turned on, and that Drew was too."

"What I felt is indescribable. The spanking part, meh that was nothing but Drew was right on when he said the psychological aspect would cream my jeans. Well, he didn't put it that way but that's the way it is. Even now, just thinking about being helpless and bare-assed across his knee makes me tingle. It's wonderful but it's scary, too.

I mean, I think this role-playing is going to go further between us. I've already been wondering what it would feel like to be tied to his bed which I just happened to notice is a four-poster—"

I interrupt excitedly saying: "Oh, and if you're tied down helpless and spreadeagled he could use The Bumblebee on you and drive you crazy!"

"The *what!?*"

"Oh, I didn't tell you about that? about my special night? I will but later, later, I want to hear about you and Drew first."

"Okay. Anyhow, a bondage thing - how much would you have to trust somebody to let them make you that vulnerable?"

"Honestly? I'm certain you'd be 100 percent safe with Drew because I'm pretty sure he's in love with you."

"Yes, I know he is."

"Wow! your ego is showing."

"No," she laughs, "He told me he loved me. And I could tell he meant it. But he also acknowledged, thanks to you and I do thank you for this, that he knows I'm not looking for any kind of commitment. He said he'll commit to me anyways but won't have any expectations in return."

"See, he does love you. And you're lucky because he's such a smart man who really understands feelings and all the emotions and stuff."

"Mmm. Mind, he also said that if I ever manage to push him to his limits he'll definitely spank me within an inch of my life."

"Oooohhh!"

"That's what I said! And then I told him that I've got half-a-mind to test that claim... someday!"

"So, sounds like you're all ready for tonight's fun-and-games?"

"With bells on!"

Chapter Eight

Drew

I never did get a chance to talk to Jane but I think - hope - she'll be okay with everything. When the guys got back last night they did demand to hear every detail but Brent also said that they'd had a good night out which means Jane did too.

I have to confess that I held back on the more emotional parts of my evening. My professing everlasting love... I'm not ready to share that with them.

We still have our first special adventure coming up in an hour or so, and I'm sure we'll have more of them in the near future. Maybe we'll spend a couple of months with each other but it's not going to last forever. Meanwhile, there's no need for me to intrude my emotions into our time together.

I don't want Brent and Harry feeling awkward and holding back because truly I'm not jealous. I'm going to have to figure that out because it's strange... I can only imagine it's because the three of us have always been so close and always on the same wave-length. Part of it is because of our experience with Jane felt so right, so natural. Olivia deserves to enjoy that experience as well.

However, I really enjoyed describing my physical session with Livy. Telling them how inviting her bare bottom is, how her breasts are firm yet soft, how a man could drown in her kisses. After our trip to the strip-club they already know that her body is totally hairless but I had them entranced with my description of how it feels to touch (velvety) and how it feels to fuck (slippery) a shaved pussy.

We're definitely primed for tonight.

However, I really enjoyed describing my physical session with Livy. Telling them how inviting her bare bottom is, how her breasts are firm yet soft, how a man could drown in her kisses.

After our trip to the strip-club they already know that her body is totally hairless but I had them entranced with my description of how it feels to touch (velvety) and how it feels to fuck (slippery) a shaved pussy.

We're definitely primed for tonight.

Harry

I feel like I just lived through the longest day of my life. In fact, the longest 24 hours! The girls should be arriving any minute now and all I can say is FINALLY!!!

I swear I got such a hard-on just listening to Drew last night when he talked about fucking Livy. I thought my balls would explode when he talked about touching and fucking her bare pussy. Waxed? or shaved? I wonder if she does or herself or goes to some place to get it done? Are there such places? and if so, how do I get a job there?

Livy, Livy, Livy. I keep seeing her on that stage. She's a born performer and oh God she is so fuckable.

Funny, but when we talk about Jane our conversation is loving but with Livy it's just pure unadulterated sexy, sexy-sex. I guess Jane is the girl-next-door, sweet and fun, while Livy is the girl on the silver screen, exotic and erotic.

The contrast between Olivia Carstairs and Miss Kitty is such a turn-on. Livy is definitely my dream girl. I can't wait to get my hands on her body,

I can't wait to see her bright smiling face, I can't wait to be inside her, and I've had to wait all fucking day!

Livy

From the moment we arrive and all five of us are standing around in the living-room I know I have to take charge of the proceedings. We're all eager to begin but nobody seems to know how to start.

Luckily for them I've already written the script in my head. So, I get them seated while I take the stage, so to speak, and deliver my lines.

"You know, when Jane told me about her first special adventure I made her start at the very beginning and take me through it step-by-step. I was playing it out in my mind but I still had her act out a few bits to show me.

Anyhow, she talked about being pulled back against you Harry, after you'd already undone her halter at the top but her chest was still covered up at that point. She demonstrated and then told me about Brent untying the bow which made the material fall open, exposing her bare breasts, so I untied the bow and saw what you guys saw, but Jane was uncomfortable. She immediately got up and put on another top. I didn't say anything at the time but Jane, I really wanted to fondle your breasts because they're beautiful."

I look from one to another and see they're all hanging off every word.

I was envious of the great experience you'd had, I was still in shock that it happened period! and I was very, very curious.

I know how my own breasts feel, and at the club whenever one of the girls has implants done – as most of them do – they go around asking us all to rub and squeeze to make sure everything feels okay. So I've fondled breasts before but I really wanted to touch yours.

Of course I was a little bit angry and I might have pinched them too, so maybe it was just as well that you moved away all *Miss Modesty*.

Sometimes I've wondered if I'm a lesbian but I'm like 99 percent sure that I'm not. I've had plenty of opportunities with my fellow dancers but although they're very pretty and walking around naked all the time I've never felt any physical attraction.

Sooo, the point of all this is to say I want to be the one to undress Jane, if that's okay?"

And of course they agree, as I knew they would. They're happy to have me as emcee to start the evening, and they're turned on to think of me stripping and caressing Jane while they watch.

"Oh yes, yes that's so okay, Olivia! It's totally, totally okay. I've been hoping to see this very thing!" enthuses Harry. He's gotten himself so worked up and is so keen that I hope he doesn't end up disappointed.

Jane doesn't say anything but I see her flash a quick look at Brent. He sits back in his chair totally relaxed and with a smile on his face, ready to enjoy the show. I can't interpret the look Drew gives me.

I pull Jane up from the sofa-bed and position her where everyone can see us. I look at what she's wearing, it's definitely an improvement, and give her bonus points for choosing this particular dress. It's plain but has about twenty buttons down the front so stripping her bare will take some time, and I know all about building the anticipation.

I start with the bottom button, at waist level, and work my way up. The dress has spaghetti straps so she isn't wearing a bra and by time I've undone about half the buttons I can see Jane's nipples poking through the lightweight summer material.

She hasn't said a word but her teeth are worrying away at her bottom lip and I know what that signifies. I also know it's a gesture that drives men crazy.

Finally I'm at the last button which I undo slowly. The bodice of the dress gapes open but only a bit of cleavage is showing. I pull the skinny straps down her arms – making sure that my long nails lightly stroke her skin – baring her all the way to her hips then I push the dress to the floor and she steps out of it.

Jane's breasts are bigger than mine. They're lovely and full and tilt upwards. Her nipples are red at the moment but I suspect the usual color is pink. I exhale blowing a deep breath across her chest and enjoy seeing her skin tighten with goosebumps, her tits quivering slightly. That's a trick one of the strippers taught me.

Jane has a curvy figure. Her waist tucks in and her hips are rounded. Being taller I can easily take hold of her wrists to raise her arms above her head while I slowly spin her around giving each of the men a good look.

Her breasts lift even higher when her arms are in this position. I pull her up on her tiptoes and that adds to the already appealing shape of her bottom, bared by her thong.

I move her over to Brent's chair and when I nudge his knee he understands my intention and spreads his legs apart. I sit Jane in the space with her back to his chest and tilt her against him. Then I wrap his hands around her wrists and pull them up so that he's lifting her arms to fold his behind his head. Now she's our captive, unprotected and utterly delectable.

Kneeling on the floor in front of her puts my eyes at the level of her perfect tits. I reach out and touch them gently, caressing and massaging. Her nipples are like little pebbles. I rub them between my fingers and thumbs, both nipples at the same time. I feel her breasts swell against my hand. Her skin is incredibly soft.

Jane still hasn't said a word but despite her blush she's arched her back and is starting to squirm. Brent has bent his head to rest alongside her neck with his eyes avidly watching what my hands are doing to her. I can hear Harry groan and I know he's leaning forward to get an eyeful.

Finally, I risk a glance over my shoulder at Drew who isn't looking at Jane, he's looking at me. I think I know what that look means and my body gives an involuntary shiver.

Turning back to Jane I run a long-nailed finger down the front of her thong. Her wetness shows in a darker stain on the fabric. I get to my feet in one fluid motion and smoothly pull off her thong as I straighten up.

Now she's completely naked, the only one of us who is, and she's lying in Brent's arms fully exposed to all of our eyes. He kisses her neck and when I tuck the damp thong into his shirt pocket Jane gives a little gasp.

Her flushed chest is heaving with each rapid breath, she's almost panting. I tug her thighs open just enough to show that my little Janey is fully, visibly aroused. I half-expect to hear applause before realizing this isn't my show. I make a flamboyant gesture to Brent to enjoy his prize.

Brent immediately turns Jane around so she's curled up in his lap and they kiss deeply while his hands travel all over her from her hair to her legs, stroking and squeezing her body, and she is doing the same to him. The sounds coming from the two of them making out is a real turn-on to us watching.

By ignoring me and immersing himself in Jane's embrace Brent is making his choice clear. I know he and I will make love later – we all will – but he's shown his preference and Jane will blossom because of it.

I admit to a slight twinge of jealousy - he's *so* good-looking - but I'm relieved that Jane hasn't been left out. This will make things easier for all of us going forward.

Harry stands up and grabs my hand saying: "I wanted you to give me a lap-dance, Livy, but I can't wait a moment longer."

I let him push me down on the sofa-bed and only undressing as much as necessary he's entering me from behind. I'm still a little sore from my time with Drew last night but playing with Jane has lubricated me and I'm soon taking in every inch with pleasure.

Drew comes over and strips me so Harry can fondle my breasts. He squeezes and sighs with contentment. Then Harry pulls off his shorts with one hand and tilts us over until we're lying on our sides but still connected while he pumps and I push back with a wiggle.

Drew is lying down now too, facing me so we can stare into each other's eyes. I've got Harry holding me by my tits while pounding my pussy, and Drew kisses me then reaches down to tease my clit. The sensations I feel racing through my body are fantastic.

I gasp with surprise when an orgasm catches me, crying out: "I can't believe how I've wasted the last ten years!"

Jane cries out too shortly after that and I see that she's now straddled Brent and is riding him with passion. Her head is thrown back and he's nuzzling her breast. Our eyes meet and she returns my smile. Friends again.

Later Jane comments: "This is like playing naked Twister!" as Drew pulls her across all our bodies sharing the sofa-bed so they can enjoy a turn with each other.

When they cuddle afterwards I insinuate myself in between them and kiss each one in turn. The three of us lie close together, caressing and kissing, then Drew claims me for a hard, fast fuck while Brent pulls Jane back into his arms.

I've already been with Brent – wonderful - such an enthusiastic lover. And am now spreading my legs for another go with Harry, having worn Drew out. I suspect I'm going to be walking bowlegged tomorrow!

He gives me a lazy smile and settles comfortably to watch us.

Harry is a very satisfying lover, careful to ensure his partner's satisfaction, and although he's reveling in being with me he doesn't make me feel that I'm especially special to him, not the way Drew can.

Harry does adore my hairless vagina. He keeps cupping it in his hand then stroking it with his fingers. He loves how exposed my clitoris is, and drives me mad with desire as he laps with his powerful tongue.

But after looking at Jane's strip of curling hair I think I might let mine grow out a bit. Might as well let everyone see that I'm a natural blonde.

I seem to recall that Drew is the one who did her shaping and I know he'll enjoy giving me a barbering session. How can I suggest that he make me beg for it?

His eyes are half-closed with lust as he watches me explode in Harry's mouth. I feel an overwhelming urge to taste Drew and kneeling grab hold of his dick. Harry scoots over beside us so I can hold each man's cock while I move my head back and forth from one to the other.

Jane presses up against my back, her arms reaching around my waist to hold me tight while Brent stretches over her to grab my tits. She's kissing my neck and I can hear him kissing hers. Hickeys all 'round! I think and start to laugh. Soon we're all chuckling and giggling uncontrollably.

Chapter Nine

Jane

Our first night together was perfect with everything going so much better than I expected. I wasn't pushed aside by Livy stealing all the attention. In fact, she started things off by focusing on me and I got turned on right away. I guess I'm a bit of an exhibitionist too because I loved having the guys staring at my naked body.

I appreciated that both Brent and Drew were making a special effort on my behalf but Harry was refreshing as his usual horny self.

Grabbing my breasts he stuck his face in between exclaiming: "I missed these two!" as he squeezed them tight against his cheeks.

I'm not at all anxious for this, our second time, because I'm an equal participant in our special adventures. I even feel it's okay to initiate a game of my own. Tonight I'm going to play the role of emcee and Livy will be my guinea pig.

Drew

Jane's a little devil and I love the way she thinks! She's enlisted my help to enact a vengeful plot against Livy that is guaranteed to give my girl mind-blowing orgasms... eventually. I just have to provide the props and vocal encouragement.

Livy gets aroused by humiliation and dominance, I made that discovery when I had her across my knee for a naughty-girl spanking, so Jane's plan should send Livy's libido right off the charts. I can't wait to see my girl panting and begging for release. God knows she's teased the hell out of me often enough.

Harry

"Thanks for choosing me to make the first suggestion, Jane. Give me a minute to decide where to begin..."

I make a production of pretending to think but I can't hide my grin as I consider my next move.

Tonight's playtime is meant to give everyone a turn at acting out a fantasy. Actually, we've got all weekend so we should be able to get to everyone. Jane decided I should start.

"Right! Now that we've all stripped off I'd like to see some girl-on-girl action with you and Livy."

Jane straddles Livy who is sitting on the couch. She lifts Livy's arms above her head saying: "Sounds good to me but I'd like to add a little twist to that. You see, I happen to know that Livy has a secret yearning to experiment with bondage. So I think we should restrain her."

Livy protests saying: "Oh that was private, Jane! I don't think—" but she's trapped under Jane's body and unable to escape.

"Great idea, Jane," interrupts Drew. "My bedroom's fully equipped but too small for all of us so we'll just have to improvise. How about... this tie, one of yours Brent?"

"Yeah, go ahead and use it."

"Thanks. Okay, so Livy let's just get those wrists of yours tied together like so." Kneeling behind Livy Drew quickly secures her in the silk binding, keeping a firm grip.

Turning to me Jane says: "It's your show, Harry, so now that we've got Livy helpless tell me what you'd like to see me do to her."

I'm already hard but Jane's words and the sight of Livy on offer makes me feel like I'm going to go off like firework! I squeeze the head of my cock to hold back and direct Jane to rub Livy's tits with her own.

Jane squashes her full breasts against Livy's perky ones and when each of the girls moan with pleasure I'm sure all of us guys join in, I know I do.

"My tits have never pressed against anything so soft before! I'm used to feeling a hard, hairy chest..."

"Or a rough hand, or my own hand. This feels... so good."

They're swaying their chests, rubbing their tits sideways and up-and-down. Jane's hands are free to rove and she positions one of her nipples to tease Livy's.

"Do you like this, Harry?" she asks. When I hoarsely croak out my approval both women smirk with satisfaction.

Drew calls out to Brent to get involved by holding Jane's hands behind her back. That position thrusts her luscious D-cups out and Drew brings me into the game by suggesting I feed one of Jane's nipples into Livy's mouth.

I can't help myself, I leak some pre-cum at the sight of Livy's lips closing around Jane's hard little cherry. After watching for a bit I turn my attention to Jane's other nipple and suckle hard. I hear Jane gasp and when her head falls back Brent captures her mouth in a hungry kiss.

Drew's still holding Livy's arms above her head but his other hand has skimmed down her body to find her clit. He begins stroking and we can all hear the wet sounds of Livy's arousal.

"Tits and clits! That's what I'm talking about!"

Brent

This is the hottest thing I've ever seen, I marvel to myself unable to tear my eyes away from the spectacle of my girl rubbing her bare tits against Livy's naked body. It's all so natural and real.

I've seen live action at bachelor parties and strip clubs and I've watched plenty of porn but nothing compares to this. There's no fake moaning or acting, there's just Jane's eager touching of Olivia's body with her own.

Jane's body is perfect: womanly, curvy, soft and warm yet she's exploring Livy with a sense of wonder. Running her hands all over, tickling and pinching and caressing.

Drew has to hang on tight to Livy's wrists since she's writhing so frantically at Jane's magical touch.

Jane

What a turn-on it is with all of us caressing and kissing each other's naked flesh. I can't believe how soft Livy's boobs feel! So very soft yet firm. Mine are bigger and squishier.

Her nipples darken the harder they get and little goosebumps form all over her aureoles. I guess mine do that too. Anyhow, it feels so good rubbing against her warm, soft skin.

But I want to see Livy really squirm so I detach myself stating: "Livy's cockteased each of you guys in the past so it's time for a little payback. It's your turn to torment her—"

"JANE!!!" she cries out.

"In the nicest possible way," I add.

"Brent, that bumblebee vibrator you got is on the mantle, grab it will you?"

"Sure Drew. Who gets to do the honors?"

"Oh we're all going to have a turn," I gleefully chortle, taking the sex toy from Brent. "You two each grab a knee and hold her open. Wider... good."

With Drew holding Livy from behind and the other two spreading her legs I crouch down and get a good look up close. Livy's pink snatch is smoothly shaven. I run a finger across the mound and marvel at the softness of her bare skin. Her pussy lips are swelling under my gaze and I can both see and smell her arousal. She struggles but the guys hold her in place.

Slipping the vibrator over my finger I turn it on then lean in to touch it to her clit. Livy's reaction is immediate. She lifts her pelvis up high and begins clenching her bum, twerking and jerking, while grunting through clenched teeth.

"That's enough, Jane. Let her subside," Drew says, pushing my hand away. Livy whines indignantly but Drew just chuckles. Harry leans in to brush his nose against the swollen organ and Livy shrieks out a sharp cry.

"My turn," claims Brent and I slip the bumblebee off my finger and onto his. I'm entranced by his technique as he dips and dabs the device over Livy's pulsating clit. The cum is running down her pussy lips to drip on her thighs.

She's begging *oh please, please, please* and II shiver at the recollection of him playing me the exact same way... like I was a musical instrument he was fine-tuning.

"Pass it to Harry but Harry don't touch her yet."

"Don't worry I won't. I'll just think of all the times Livy left me with blue balls."

"No Harry touch me, touch me now, hard. I wanna cum, please Harry."

Harry groans as Livy pleads for release but holds back until Drew gives him the nod. Harry doesn't put the bumblebee on his finger, he holds it between his lips, and vibrates her with his warm mouth.

"Oh! Oh! Oh!" cries Livy and Drew allows her one orgasm that's quickly cut short. She's red-faced and gasping, her body held rigid, her exposed pussy shiny wet and throbbing.

Now Drew is using his free hand to twist Livy's nipple while he licks at her neck and orders her to *beg for cock*. I feel a great sense of satisfaction when she does.

Drew

One of the many thing I love – and often hate - about Olivia is her cool poise. She's always so controlled, methodical, and calculating in her behavior and responses. Nothing ever fazes or rattles her. But now...

Seeing Livy squirming and struggling, hearing her mewling begging cries, smelling her arousal and even a faint trace of perfumed sweat, is just mind-blowing. It's almost impossible to believe this moist, flush flesh belongs to Olivia Carstairs!

I've turned her body halfway round so I can see her blushing face, her diamond-hard nipples, and her bare, bald pussy with its swollen red folds slick with cum. With my free hand I roughly stroke her hot skin, squeezing her ass then massaging a tit. She is literally putty in my hands, weak with desire, her hunger making her so compliant in a very un-Livy-like way.

"Whine to feel my hard cock pounding you," I order and she obeys!

Keening out a litany of *please Drew, please fuck me, I need you, I need you to fuck me hard with your big cock.* I wish I could resist just a little more in order to enjoy this moment longer but my girl needs dicking down right now, and I need to man up.

Lifting up her leg I slide into that tight wetness and her fiery cunt grabs hold of my cock and squeezes. We're both talking dirty nonsense that just drives us even harder and faster. I feel cum flood her passage, soaking me, as she orgasms and I push her for another and another.

I won't be satisfied until she's wrung out and clinging, fucked into submission and aching to be soothed and cuddled and kissed.

Eventually I released her and fucked Jane while Harry screwed Livy. We all took turns with each other, slept, played some more, ate, played again... we fucked ourselves silly until we went out for another big breakfast on Sunday.

Sore, sated, and still sleepy we wolfed down our meals while smiling at each other. What a weekend!

Every moment was enjoyable, but for me the memorable part was plunging into Livy's welcoming pussy while she begged me to go as fast and as hard as I wanted.

Chapter Ten

Drew

We all knew our special adventures wouldn't – couldn't – last forever. Livy is a student of mine and as the youngest member of my department I really can't overstep the boundaries.

I did expect we'd have the summer but I didn't count on Olivia acting like... well, like Olivia. She set up a get-together but arrived without Jane. Not because Jane couldn't make it but because she wasn't invited. Talk about overstepping!

Looking back I can only guess that Jane's special adventures with the three of us made Olivia jealous. Knowing her as I do I can easily believe she wants her own turn at being the centre of attention as the only female.

When we realize what she'd planned I'm angry and even Harry gets that Olivia has gone too far.

He tries to explain it to her: "See, we want to fuck both of you, and we like to watch you two getting it on."

Brent is livid. "Jane wanted you to join us but you just want to shut her out. You're a bitch Olivia and I don't want any part of this without Jane," he declares.

"Oh Jane won't mind. Believe me, she knows I want to have my turn with you three all to myself. It's only fair," she says, blithely unconcerned that Brent is seething mad.

"You can count me out, Olivia. No Jane, no me."

"Oh Brent you don't mean that," Olivia replies with a pout.

Brent rarely loses his temper but he's close to doing so when he mimics her saying: "Oh Olivia I do mean it."

Turning to me he asks to borrow my car and I nod. He knows where I keep the keys and a minute later we hear the front slam.

Now Olivia turns to the two of us with an expression of wide-eyed innocence and a trembling lip. The little actress! I've had enough of this.

Without a word I sit down and grabbing her hand drag her across my lap. I immediately begin scolding and pulling down her short-shorts and thong start spanking her bare ass. Hard.

"You deserve this Olivia, and you know it!"

"No, Drew! Don't, not in front of Harry," she shrieks.

"Oh Harry doesn't mind, do you bro?"

He's been avidly watching the scene unfold and now he grins at me commenting: "Mind? Fuck, no! I think it's hot, kinky and hot."

"Livy's ass is going to be hot by time I'm finished."

This conversation has gone on while I've been laying down stroke after stroke. I'm not holding back and she's feeling it. Soon she's kicking her legs and putting on quite a performance of squealing and hollering but instead of easing up I double my efforts to really punish that pretty behind.

She's crying out for me to stop saying: "Drew it hurts! It stings, it stings so bad."

"This time it's supposed to hurt, Olivia. It's punishment. You know you've ruined things with Brent now, right? If he doesn't want to play anymore then Jane won't come back either."

Although we always enjoyed each other's bodies to the fullest it was obvious that Jane and Brent would eventually split off as a couple and stop attending. Livy's little stunt has forced the issue.

The realization that our special adventures have come to an abrupt end fuels my anger at Livy. I continue for at least five minutes more delivering steady smacks until her bottom is bright red and she's sobbing.

I finish and order *go suck Harry's cock*. A very subdued Olivia scurries to obey. Sitting back in the chair I rub my sore palm while staring at her ass and thinking how much worse it must feel.

Harry got very turned on watching Livy get spanked and his cock is out and ready. He's dominating her by grabbing her hair in his fist and roughly fucking her mouth, forcing his dick down her throat.

Tonight the two of us are going to enjoy trading our compliant and penitent sex toy back and forth. Instead of having three men worshiping her body Olivia is going to be used, degraded, and humiliated. I'm 100 percent certain she'll throw herself into this new role with gusto.

We'll finish the night with Olivia going over Harry's lap for his turn at punishing her for ending our fivesome. I can't wait to see his big hand spank her ass and I'll demand that she makes eye contact with me throughout her ordeal.

Brent

I'm so pissed off at Olivia I can hardly think straight. How could she? *Why* would she? What was she... arrgghh!!

I drive straight to Jane's dorm and impatiently pace in the lobby while they fetch her. I'm not allowed to go upstairs since it isn't co-ed.

The questioning look on her face turns into a bright smile when she sees me. My heart thrums and my whole body relaxes under the influence of her calming presence.

"Brent! This is a wonderful surprise...?" I hear the question in her voice but there are too many people nearby, deliberately hanging around and listening in.

"I had to see you and talk to you. Is there somewhere we can go? Not here, outside, I've got Drew's car."

"Sure, I'll just grab my purse—"

I feel I can't wait a moment longer and speak more harshly than I intended saying: "You won't need it, Jane. Let's just go now."

She's puzzled but to my relief doesn't argue instead she just moves to the door with me following closely behind. I grab hold of her hand and squeeze tight as I direct her through the foyer.

Jane

This new aspect of Brent is bringing out all my maternal instincts. Something's wrong and I just want to take him in my arms and soothe away whatever is bothering him.

I recognize Drew's car and head to the passenger door. Before I can open it Brent steps up close and embraces me in a tight hug.

We stand like that for a solid minute with Brent's face in my hair, breathing in the scent of my shampoo, until he finally says: "Just holding you makes me feel like everything will be okay. It will be okay so long as we're together."

"I don't know what you're talking about but I love hearing you say that," I tell him with a little laugh.

"Oh Jane, you feel so good and this feels so right."

He kisses me with passion and I melt into him. *Brent, my love Brent,* I think briefly before losing myself to his lips.

I don't know how long we stood there necking until a cackle and a *get a room* comment brings us round. I smile sheepishly but he doesn't smile at all, just stares into my eyes with a serious expression on his face. Then he opens the door and ushers me into the car.

"Let's grab a coffee but I've never been able to deal with those fluorescent lights so we'll just drink it in the car, okay?"

"Sure, sounds good. I agree with you about that lighting. It's not only painfully bright but it hums. So irritating."

He takes us to a popular drive-thru and we choose our coffees and a sweet snack. Parking in the back of the lot we settle with our drinks and food and when I ask what's happened he tells me what Livy's done.

My first thought is *of course she's ruined it*, and my second registers his disgust which warms me inside.

Shaking my head I tell him: "This is *so* Olivia. I knew she was jealous when I told her about that first time we were all together," we exchange happy smiles at the memory, "but I thought her joining us meant she'd moved past that. I guess not."

"Jane she's absolutely poisonous. I know that because of your self-esteem issue it wasn't easy for you to include her but you did, and you did it without complaint. She doesn't deserve your friendship."

Having Brent come to my defense like this is butterfly-inducing. I'll dissect that self-esteem remark later, for now all I can think of is how he's supporting me. I know how I feel about him but it sounds like he feels the same about me. Me! *not* beautiful Olivia but plain Jane.

My lower lip trembles heralding tears but he rescues me from the overly emotional moment saying: "Jane, stay still so I can kiss you without spilling boiling hot coffee all over us. As a lawyer I understand lawsuits and I don't want one so don't move, okay?"

Smiling I close my eyes and hold myself motionless while he bestows a tender kiss. A tender, *loving* kiss and I sigh: "Oh, Brent."

Pulling back I see the reassurance in his eyes and my searching glance turns into a happy grin. I'm not imagining this – the feeling we share is real!

"So it's over then."

"Yeah well, I can't - I won't - do anything like that with Olivia ever again. And Jane, I'd like to keep you to myself anyway."

"I'd like that too, Brent. Although I guess this means I won't be getting a spanking from Drew..." I tease.

"Well no, not from Drew," he replies, drawing out Drew's name, while smirking at me.

"I guess we knew our fun times couldn't last forever—" I begin but Brent cuts me off.

"Well, we knew our fun times couldn't last forever—" I begin but he cuts me off.

"You know, I think I'm glad this has happened. Not the way it has but well it's made me realize what you mean to me, Jane.

I was attracted to you before that first get-together, in fact I'm the one who suggested you when Harry brought up his idea. He said he'd thought of you but figured there was no way you'd be interested. Drew agreed with me and told Harry to sound you out. By the way, what exactly did he say? I did wonder—"

"He said nothing! He invited me to watch a movie on his big-screen and that was it, nothing else."

"Really? You mean it all came about naturally? Shit Jane that's... wow, that's so cool."

"Brent did you honestly think Harry invited me over for an orgy and I jumped at the chance?" I'm not sure how I feel about that. I'm not flattered but I'm not exactly angry either.

"I didn't really think about it at all. I mean, beforehand sure I was wondering how he'd get you to come over and hoping that whatever he said would work. I was so happy to see you sitting on the sofa when I came in I never thought any more about it."

I'm smiling as I say: "So the three of you plotted and came up with *Jane's Special Adventure*, hmm? What if I'd slapped your hands away when you started stripping me on the couch?"

"We'd have stopped right away. Jane, you know that, right?"

"I do, Brent. I remember how anxious you were to have me clearly give my consent. As you say, you are a lawyer after all."

"If you'd turned us down I would have had to approach you on my own which would have been so hard after being rejected... I'd have been so worried that you wanted nothing to do with me. Damn Jane, that was a close one!"

"If it had have been Drew instead of you I might have said *no* but Brent you hypnotized me with your gorgeous eyes and that was it, I was done for."

"Thank God! But you know I felt things change once Olivia joined us. Everything was still good and I loved watching you and her touching each other but it just, I don't know, it was different. Not so spontaneous maybe? Or maybe I was starting to get jealous of the guys having sex with you? Maybe? I'm not sure..."

"It's funny you saying that because after the first time, when the four of us were at breakfast I felt 100 percent attuned to you guys. Like it was the rightest, oh that's not a word, but you understand my meaning? Everything felt absolutely perfect and absolutely normal. When we all squeezed together for a photo I never for a moment wondered what the waitress thought of us, or anyone else in the place."

"Yeah, I know exactly what you mean. I felt that too, totally comfortable, I think we all felt the same."

"Right, but remember when I went to the show with you and Harry and then afterwards we were in the Food Court? Well then I started wondering what the other people there were thinking about me being with you two guys. And you know what changed?"

"That it was just three of us instead of four? That shouldn't have made a difference—"

"No, and it didn't. What changed was that Livy knew about us, what happened between us, and she'd been a bitch about it. She'd made some pretty derogatory comments about me and about us, all four of us. She like... cast a shadow over what we had. Instead of us all just being ourselves I was seeing things through her eyes, through society's eyes.

Brent, you're absolutely right. What we had couldn't continue. I mean, our parents? They'd never accept our foursome or fivesome."

He leans back against the car door and his eyes drift upwards, a sure sign he's thinking. After a moment he muses: "Our get-togethers aren't illegal but... you're right, they wouldn't be accepted. Modern love takes many forms but my family sure isn't modern! And once I started to feel possessive towards you I knew I wasn't in the right mind-set for our adventures any more."

"Self-awareness is crucial to success in any kind of relationship. Even vets and their patients," she chuckles, removing any lecturing tone from her words. "We have to know our limitations such as not being able to adopt every cute puppy or kitten or especially the senior pets we meet."

"And living in a dorm means no pets at all I take it."

"Yeah, that's a drawback for sure. My elderly cat died my first year of school and I felt so guilty for being here instead of there... I still can't consider another cat yet. I will, someday, but not yet."

He bops my nose and tells me I have a tender heart.

Harry

I'm not ashamed to be a man-whore and I'm open to try anything. I loved that first session with just me and Drew and Livy where he introduced us to all kinds of exciting new fun and games. There was something so damn hot about a submissive Olivia Carstairs.

We have no interest in finding a new girl to join us. There was something special with we three guys and Jane that I know can't be replicated. Drew talked about poly-this and poly-that and said the dynamic just didn't work out for us.

Everything is different now, and though the remaining three of us really get into each other when we play I know Drew and Livy spend a lot of time together. Just the two of them.

Drew spent time prepping Livy's ass so we could both fuck a hole together. I remember laughing at her complaints about sitting on those hard lecture hall benches with a butt-plug in but she said it was worth it. That was an incredible experience for all of us.

As promised, the grinding and the fullness of double penetration took her to new heights of pleasure. I'd never known how tight the butt-hole is and holy shit, what a sensation. Drew knows a lot about this BDSM stuff and Livy trusts him. Unfortunately more and more time passes between our get-togethers.

Miss Kitty retired once Olivia started getting acting jobs and the threat of discovery became too much of a risk. Her work takes her to different shooting locations and she's often gone for weeks at a time. Livy worked really hard to get to where she is so naturally I'm happy that she's doing so well but...

Drew is content to wait for Livy's return trips home. He isn't interested in meeting anyone else and never dates, that I know of.

He saved up his money and bought out Brent's share of our home so that he and Jane could get their own place. Of course Brent gave him a good price and, I guess, some day I will do the same.

I visited Brent and Jane at their new home and checked to see if they have a bathtub. They do! and based on Brent's smirk he figured out what I was thinking. I know he and Jane will act out that messy fantasy we had way back when but this time it will be just the two of them.

Drew's not-so-secret secret is that Livy still has, and always will have, complete power over him. Their game of domination and submission has ventured into *a deeper commitment and understanding*, as he puts it, but he no longer shares details of the specifics. What a disappointment!

I enjoyed exploring with Drew and Livy, people I know and trust. Seeing Olivia crawling across the floor is fucking hot, and having her drip hot candle wax on my ass? major hard-on! But it was only playtime for me, I just can't get into that lifestyle.

Me? I love the ladies and now that our *fivesome* is no longer happening I'm free to enjoy variety. I know I'll never meet men who I can trust like Drew and Brent, our friendship has been thirty years in the making. So no more group sex unless it's me with some horny women!

No more special adventures unless I can put something together with women from the gym - some of them are up for anything. Maybe I can still live out my fantasy of a *menage a trois* – with me being the main attraction, of course!

None of that crowd is into *exclusive shit*. I figure that's what happens when you're obsessed with your own body, it's like it's easier to get off on other people's bodies too.

I'm not a bit shy about sharing my attraction to shaved pussies and so far my dates have all been happy to please me, knowing that I'll be sure to please them. That's what it's all about, for now anyway.

I'm sure I'll meet somebody someday and when I do I'll be bringing a lot of experience and technique to her bed. Guess I better not get to specific about how I learned, lots of women get jealous about shit like that.

The fur-mommies I date, who I meet at the animal clinic, don't know about each other. Probably a mistake that could get messy and bring about a very unwelcome complication but hey, a man has to have some secrets, right?

I suppose my best-kept secret is the identity of Miss Kitty but actually it's not. No, instead my guilty secret is how often I fantasize over that first time with the guys and Jane. Her sweetness along with the rapport, the brotherhood, and the camaraderie was perfection.

I think about that night a lot. Jane's adventure turned out to be oh-so-special for all of us.

Don't miss out!

Visit the website below and you can sign up to receive emails whenever Lori Laidlaw publishes a new book. There's no charge and no obligation.

https://books2read.com/r/B-A-RDEBB-FEEAD

BOOKS 2 READ

Connecting independent readers to independent writers.

Also by Lori Laidlaw

Alpha + Omega Wolf-Shifters
Dominant + Violent + Hot = An Alpha Male
Her Claiming Bite = True Love

Standalone
Lockdown + 3 Alphas = Heat: An Omega's Thrilling Dark Romantic
Adventure
Girlie: Undeniable Attraction Enemies to Lovers Steamy Standalone
Cruel Obligation
Jane's Special Adventure
Captive's Deception
Finn and Marbeth
"Princess Weds Killer" = Fake News

Watch for more at https://lorilaidlaw.com.

About the Author

Lori says:

I love the fun and excitement in the Adult Romance genre and all of its sub-categories. It's such fun to write!

I'm half in love with all of my characters... and their moods range from playful to dangerous and everything in between!

The men are unfeeling and cruel until the innocent heroine melts the ice from their hearts and turns them into OTT possessive touch-her-and-die alphas.

My stories are multiple POV expressing mature themes and passionate encounters with enough steam to stimulate your imagination.

It's all about the love.

Email: AuthorLoriLaidlaw@gmail.com

Website: https://lorilaidlaw.com

Bluesky: https://bsky.app/profile/lorilaidlaw.bsky.social

Facebook: https://www.facebook.com/people/Author-Lori-Laidlaw/61555470454210/

Goodreads: https://www.goodreads.com/author/show/29566696.Lori_Laidlaw

Read more at https://lorilaidlaw.com.